DINOSAURS

Unearthing the Secrets of Ancient Beasts

These and other books are included in the
Encyclopedia of Discovery and Invention series:

Airplanes
Anesthetics
Animation
Atoms
Automobiles
Clocks
Computers
Dinosaurs
Explosives
Genetics
Germs
Gravity
Guns
Human Origins
Lasers
Maps

Microscopes
Movies
Phonograph
Photography
Plastics
Plate Tectonics
Printing Press
Radar
Radios
Railroads
Ships
Submarines
Telephones
Telescopes
Television
Vaccines

DINOSAURS
Unearthing the Secrets of Ancient Beasts

by DON NARDO

The ENCYCLOPEDIA of
D·I·S·C·O·V·E·R·Y
and **INVENTION**

P.O. Box 289011 SAN DIEGO, CA 92198-9011

Library of Congress Cataloging-in-Publication Data

Nardo, Don, 1947-
  Dinosaurs: unearthing the secrets of ancient beasts / by Don
Nardo.

    p. cm.—(The Encyclopedia of discovery and invention)
  Includes bibliographical references and index.
  ISBN 1-56006-253-3
  1. Dinosaurs—Juvenile literature.   [1. Dinosaurs.]   I. Title.
II. Series.
QE862.D5N373   1995
567.9′1—dc20   94-10958
                                                        CIP
                                                        AC

Contents

Foreword 7

Introduction 10

CHAPTER 1 ■ Before Noah: Fossil Teeth
and Dragon Bones 12

    Early discoveries;
    Biblical explanations;
    Nineteenth-century studies;
    Naming the beasts.

CHAPTER 2 ■ Bone Wars: The First Great Age
of Discovery 22

    Public interest grows;
    The Race for new discoveries;
    Developing field methods.

CHAPTER 3 ■ Desert Quest: Creatures of the
Flaming Cliffs 32

    Dinosaurs around the world;
    Absolute dating;
    The Gobi expedition.

CHAPTER 4 ■ Terrible Claw: A Cold Look at
Warm Blood 42

    Studying what makes dinosaurs tick;
    Evidence to support warm-blooded theory;
    The debate rages on.

CHAPTER 5 ■ Avian Ancestry: The Case for Flying
Dinosaurs 51

    Feathers, wings, and wishbones;
    The world's first bird;
    The origins of flight.

CHAPTER 6 ■ Good Mother: Social Life in a
Mud Nest   59
    The Two Medicine babies;
    A new view of dinosaur behavior;
    Hunting in packs;
    Dinosaur communication.

CHAPTER 7 ■ Cosmic Intruder: The K-T Event and
the Dinosaurs' Demise   68
    A sudden death;
    Arguments and counterarguments;
    The mysterious clay layer;
    Nuclear winter;
    The "smoking gun."

CHAPTER 8 ■ Future Hunting: Dinosaurs at
the Poles and Beyond   76
    Today's dinosaur hunters;
    New techniques and new finds;
    Polar dinosaurs;
    The Search for knowledge continues.

Glossary   85
For Further Reading   87
Works Consulted   89
Index   91
About the Author   95
Picture Credits   96

Foreword

The belief in progress has been one of the dominant forces in Western Civilization from the Scientific Revolution of the seventeenth century to the present. Embodied in the idea of progress is the conviction that each generation will be better off than the one that preceded it. Eventually, all peoples will benefit from and share in this better world. R.R. Palmer, in his *History of the Modern World*, calls this belief in progress "a kind of nonreligious faith that the conditions of human life" will continually improve as time goes on.

For over a thousand years prior to the seventeenth century, science had progressed little. Inquiry was largely discouraged, and experimentation, almost nonexistent. As a result, science became regressive and discovery was ignored. Benjamin Farrington, a historian of science, characterized it this way: "Science had failed to become a real force in the life of society. Instead there had arisen a conception of science as a cycle of liberal studies for a privileged minority. Science ceased to be a means of transforming the conditions of life." In short, had this intellectual climate continued, humanity's future would have been little more than a clone of its past.

Fortunately, these circumstances were not destined to last. By the seventeenth and eighteenth centuries, Western society was undergoing radical and favorable changes. And the changes that occurred gave rise to the notion that progress was a real force urging civilization forward. Surpluses of consumer goods were replacing substandard living conditions in most of Western Europe. Rigid class systems were giving way to social mobility. In nations like France and the United States, the lofty principles of democracy and popular sovereignty were being painted in broad, gilded strokes over the fading canvases of monarchy and despotism.

But more significant than these social, economic, and political changes, the new age witnessed a rebirth of science. Centuries of scientific stagnation began crumbling before a spirit of scientific inquiry that spawned undreamed of technological advances. And it was the discoveries and inventions of scores of men and women that fueled these new technologies, dramatically increasing the ability of humankind to control nature—and, many believed, eventually to guide it.

It is a truism of science and technology that the results derived from observation and experimentation are not finalities. They are part of a process. Each discovery is but one piece in a continuum bridging past and present and heralding an extraordinary future. The heroic age of the Scientific Revolution was simply a start. It laid a foundation upon which succeeding generations of imaginative thinkers could build. It kindled the belief that progress is possible as long as there were gifted men and women who would respond to society's needs. When Antonie van Leeuwenhoek observed *Animalcules* (little animals) through his high-powered microscope in 1683, the discovery did not end there. Others followed who would call these "little animals" bacteria and, in time, recognize their role in the process of health and disease. Robert Koch, a German bacteriologist and winner of the Nobel Prize in Physiology and Medicine, was one of these men. Koch firmly established that bacteria are responsible for causing infectious diseases. He identified, among others, the causative organisms of anthrax and tuberculosis. Alexander Fleming, another Nobel Laureate, progressed still further in the quest to understand and control bacteria. In 1928, Fleming discovered penicillin, the antibiotic wonder drug. Penicillin, and the generations of antibiotics that succeeded it, have done more to prevent premature death than any other discovery in the history of humankind. And as civilization hastens toward the twenty-first century, most agree that the conquest of van Leeuwenhoek's "little animals" will continue.

The *Encyclopedia of Discovery and Invention* examines those discoveries and inventions that have had a sweeping impact on life and thought in the modern world. Each book explores the ideas that led to the invention or discovery, and, more importantly, how the world changed and continues to change because of it. The series also highlights the people behind the achievements—the unique men and women whose singular genius and rich imagination have altered the lives of everyone. Enhanced by photographs and clearly explained technical drawings, these books are comprehensive examinations of the building blocks of human progress.

DINOSAURS

Unearthing the Secrets of Ancient Beasts

DINOSAURS

Introduction

Despite the widespread popularity of and fascination for dinosaurs, surprisingly few people can explain, in scientific terms, what these ancient beasts were. Indeed, popular misconceptions about dinosaurs abound. A typical assumption, for instance, is that all huge prehistoric species, or specific kinds of animals, were dinosaurs. This idea is incorrect on two counts. First, not all dinosaurs were huge. Some were about the size of humans and many were as small as dogs or chickens.

Second, dinosaurs were only one of many kinds of creatures, both large and small, that inhabited the earth in past ages. In this regard, the term *prehistoric*, referring to all ages before the advent of human civilization, can be misleading. Dinosaurs did not exist all through prehistoric times; rather, they flourished only during a particular span of about 160 million years. Scientists call this era, which lasted from about 225 to 65 million years ago, the Mesozoic, or era of "middle life." Experts divide the Mesozoic into three periods—the Triassic, Jurassic, and Cretaceous—each of which had its own distinct species of dinosaurs. Therefore, the numerous creatures that lived before and after the Mesozoic era were not dinosaurs.

Even many of the species that existed *in* the Mesozoic era were not dinosaurs. What, then, made dinosaurs unique from other Mesozoic species? For one thing, dinosaurs were reptiles. Reptiles are for the most part cold-blooded animals who bear their young by laying eggs. This made dinosaurs distinctly different from mammals, which are largely warm-blooded creatures that bear live offspring. Small mouse- and squirrel-sized mammals coexisted with dinosaurs all through Mesozoic times. Other nonreptilian ani-

... TIMELINE: DINOSAURS

1 > 2 > 3 > 4 > 5 > 6 > 7 > 8 > 9 > 10

B.C.

1 ■ ca. 4.6 billion
The earth forms.

2 ■ ca. 225 million
Beginning of Mesozoic era and Triassic period; the first dinosaurs appear.

3 ■ ca. 200 million
End of Triassic, beginning of Jurassic period.

4 ■ ca. 135 million
End of Jurassic, beginning of Cretaceous period.

5 ■ ca. 65 million
End of Cretaceous period and Mesozoic era; all dinosaurs become extinct.

A.D.

6 ■ 1650
Using biblical references, Bishop James Ussher calculates that God created the earth in 4004 B.C.

7 ■ 1677
Large thighbone discovered in Oxfordshire, England, is declared to be from a giant human who died in Noah's flood.

8 ■ 1770
Remains of *Mosasaurus*, a large marine reptile, found in a Netherlands chalk quarry.

9 ■ 1796
French scientist Georges Cuvier announces his theory of natural extinctions.

10 ■ 1825
English doctor and fossil collector Gideon Mantell names and describes *Iguanodon*, a large, prehistoric, herbivorous reptile.

11 ■ 1838
Scottish scientist Charles Lyell coins the term *paleontology* to describe the new study of ancient plants and animals.

12 ■ 1841
English anatomist Richard Owen coins the term *dinosaur*.

13 ■ 1861
First skeleton of *Archaeopteryx*, the first known bird, found in a German limestone quarry.

mals, such as fish, amphibians, and insects, shared Mesozoic landscapes with dinosaurs.

Yet simply classifying dinosaurs as reptiles is not enough, for many Mesozoic reptiles were not dinosaurs. Contrary to some popular depictions, for example, the giant flying reptiles—the bat-winged pterosaurs with wingspreads of twenty, thirty, or more feet—were not dinosaurs. Neither were the sleek, flippered, long-necked plesiosaurs and other huge aquatic monsters that hunted in the warm Mesozoic seas. And crocodiles, another group of Mesozoic reptilian species, one that survived to the present, were certainly not dinosaurs.

In fact, dinosaurs were a very specific kind of Mesozoic reptile. What set them apart was not their size, their body temperature, or their method of reproduction. Instead, it was their posture. More specifically, what made a dinosaur a dinosaur was the way it carried itself on its legs.

Most reptiles—lizards, crocodiles, and turtles, for instance—have legs that project outward from their sides so that they drag their bellies on the ground as they walk. This makes them relatively awkward and slow moving. By contrast, dinosaurs were land reptiles that walked with their legs directly beneath their bodies, much like birds, dogs, and humans. This gave dinosaurs more upright posture and with it more speed and mobility, better enabling them to search out and chase down their prey. Consequently, they were wide-ranging and highly efficient hunters. It is hardly surprising that they dominated the Mesozoic's tiny mammals and slower-moving reptiles and ruled the world's land surfaces for so many millions of years. For dinosaurs, therefore, good posture spelled success, and in a very real sense their walk was worse than their bite.

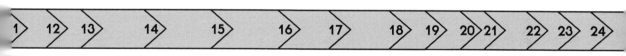

14 ■ 1877
Digging begins at Como Bluff, Wyoming, the richest fossil dinosaur site ever discovered.

15 ■ 1905–1910
Introduction of the technique of absolute dating, which measures the rate of radioactive decay in chemical isotopes.

16 ■ 1922
American naturalist Roy Chapman Andrews launches a world-famous fossil-hunting expedition into Mongolia's Gobi desert.

17 ■ 1947
American paleontologist Edwin Colbert discovers several complete skeletons of *Coelophysis*, a small carnivorous dinosaur.

18 ■ 1964
American paleontologist John Ostrom finds the remains of *Deinonychus*, or "terrible claw," which launches the modern debate over warm- versus cold-blooded dinosaurs.

19 ■ 1978
Controversial American paleontologist Robert Bakker champions the idea of warm-blooded dinosaurs; fossil hunter John Ostrom discovers nests containing the fossils of young dinosaurs in Montana.

20 ■ 1979
Scientists Luis and Walter Alvarez announce the discovery of evidence suggesting a comet or asteroid caused the death of the dinosaurs.

21 ■ 1984
John Ostrom finds the remains of a huge herd of herbivorous dinosaurs in Montana.

22 ■ 1989
Evidence begins to mount that the cosmic object that wiped out the dinosaurs fell in the Caribbean Sea.

23 ■ 1991
A Caribbean impact crater is confirmed near the coast of Mexico's Yucatan peninsula; American paleontologist David Gillette names *Seismosaurus*, the longest known dinosaur.

24 ■ 1994
Work continues at Dinosaur Cove in southeastern Australia, site of the discovery of several species of dinosaurs that were able to adapt to polar conditions.

Before Noah: Fossil Teeth and Dragon Bones

Modern scientists have identified and named about three hundred kinds of dinosaurs so far, and each year a few more dinosaur species come to light. In addition to describing the physical characteristics of dinosaurs, researchers regularly offer fresh insights into dinosaur life and behavior. The ways that dinosaurs evolved, bore and tended their young, foraged and hunted for food, and ultimately died out are becoming increasingly clear. Through books, magazines, and TV, these discoveries and theories reach the public, which has a keen and ongoing fascination for dinosaurs.

With all the scientific and popular attention paid to dinosaurs, it is easy to forget that people have known about these ancient beasts for only a little more than a century and a half. Not un-til the 1820s did scientists, mainly in Europe, begin to recognize the existence of this previously unknown group of prehistoric reptiles. And serious naming and study of dinosaurs did not start until the 1840s. Scientists' failure to identify dinosaurs earlier was not due to lack of evidence. In fact, unusual fossil bones and teeth had been unearthed long before the nineteenth century. (At the time, people referred to any old artifact or relic dug out of the ground as a fossil.) For example, people in Europe and Asia had been collecting and selling large fossil teeth, apparently reptilian in nature, since at least the 1500s. Among many other fossils of unknown origin was a large thighbone unearthed in Oxfordshire, England, in 1677. But no one at that time suspected the true nature of these relics.

In this drawing, first printed in fossil hunter Gideon Mantell's Illustrations of the Geology of Sussex, *quarry workers discover the remains of* Iguanodon, *one of the first known dinosaurs.*

Sticking to Scripture

What initially kept scientists from correctly identifying dinosaur remains was their rejection of the idea of extinction. They refused to accept that an animal species could exist and then become extinct, or die out for good. Various fossils seemed to come from unknown animals. But this did not necessarily indicate that these animals had lived and then become extinct. Perhaps, some scientists suggested, their descendants had migrated away from Europe and still existed in unexplored regions of the earth. Or perhaps the fossils had come from freaks of nature, unusually large or deformed versions of known animals.

This flat rejection of extinction came from the scientists' automatic acceptance of religious explanations for the creation of the world and animal species. Before the nineteenth century, Europeans strictly adhered to the teachings of the Bible. They saw this document as the direct word of God and thus as infallible. The Bible clearly described the stages in which God had created the heavens, the earth, plants, animals, and humans. To suggest an alternate explanation for creation was considered blasphemous, or against God, and therefore unthinkable.

The idea of extinction was also unthinkable because it did not fit into the biblical explanation of creation. According to the biblical book of Ecclesiastes, "whatsoever God doeth, it shall be forever: Nothing can be put to it, nor any thing taken from it." The meaning of this passage seemed all too clear. God's handiwork, including animals, was meant to last forever and no new

Protestant theologian James Ussher, who advocated that the earth was only a few thousand years old.

species could be created without His intervention. Neither could species die out unless He willed it, so the naturally occurring extinction of a species appeared to be impossible.

Another factor that kept scientists from recognizing the true nature of dinosaur fossils was their ignorance about the ages of both the fossils and the earth itself. The concept of strange animal species roaming the earth millions of years ago did not initially occur to people because of the widespread belief that the earth was only a few thousand years old. This belief also stemmed from biblical interpretations. Most people unquestioningly accepted the calculations of seventeenth-century Protestant theologian James Ussher. According to Pulitzer Prize-winning scholar John Noble Wilford:

Ussher, the archbishop of Armagh in the Church of Ireland, was a devoted scholar of the *Bible*, the one book he knew and valued above all others. He harbored no doubt whatsoever of the *Bible's* historical accuracy. Accordingly, he pored through the genealogies of the Old Testament, the lists of who begat whom, and made calculations of the length of each generation of the many patriarchs, priests, judges, and kings. In so working his way back through time, Ussher determined to his satisfaction that the Creation must have occurred in 4004 B.C. and the [Great] Flood in 2349 B.C. This he published in 1650.

A few years after Ussher published his work, noted English Scholar John Lightfoot confirmed the bishop's calculations and issued a refined version. According to Lightfoot, the creation had occurred at 9:00 A.M. on Sunday, October 23, 4004 B.C.!

Thus, for many years scientists had to make their observations of nature conform to the accepted orthodox view that the world was only about six thousand years old. This did not stop some from suspecting a much older earth. All around them—in fossils, in sea sediments, in rock layers beneath the ground—scholars increasingly saw evidence that the earth was in fact very ancient. But so strong was religion's hold on society that some scientists ignored this evidence outright. The eighteenth-century Swedish botanist Carolus Linnaeus, for instance, suspected an older earth, then dismissed the idea, saying, "the Scriptures do not allow this."

Other scholars tried to reconcile the geologic evidence with biblical statements. They suggested that the world was indeed much older than Bishop Ussher had decreed but that

A typical depiction of the world's animals marching two-by-two, a male and female of each species, into Noah's ark.

God had not revealed this in the Bible. According to this view, God had originally created certain species and then destroyed them in the Great Flood. By keeping Noah from preserving these animals on the ark, God brought about their extinction for His own reasons. The idea of divinely inspired extinction seemed more acceptable, so it became fashionable to identify various fossils as remnants of the world before Noah. One common view was that large reptilian teeth belonged to the dragons of mythology, which once had actually walked the earth, only to be exterminated by God. Similar was the popular notion that certain large fossil leg and arm bones came from a race of giant people mentioned in the Bible. For example, in 1677 English chemistry professor Robert Plot declared that the

The French anatomist Baron Georges Cuvier (1769-1832), whose work helped bring about scientific acceptance of the process of natural extinction.

thighbone discovered in Oxfordshire the year before had come from a giant who perished in Noah's flood.

Whole Races Extinguished

By the late eighteenth century, however, evidence that extinction was a natural rather than a divine phenomenon was beginning to mount. The first scientist to champion the idea of natural extinction was the French anatomist Baron Georges Cuvier. At an important scientific conference in 1796, Cuvier announced his view that extinctions had occurred regularly and frequently in the past. As evidence, he cited the recent discovery of a *Paleotherium* fossil, a smaller version of modern horses. Because the *Paleotherium* no longer exists, said Cuvier, it must have become extinct. Cuvier also reported that fossil elephants found beneath the streets of Paris were anatomically different from modern elephants native to Africa and India. The Parisian elephant, he insisted, had also become extinct.

Even more interesting to Cuvier was the apparent existence of large extinct reptiles. In 1770, workers at a chalk quarry in the Netherlands found a fossil set of jaws over three feet long. When French soldiers brought the jaws to Paris in the 1790s, Cuvier examined them and immediately recognized that they belonged to a huge marine, or sea-dwelling, reptile. A colleague later named the creature *Mosasaurus*. Because the *Mosasaurus* bore little resemblance

Workers at a chalk quarry in the Netherlands unearth the fossil jaws of Mosasaurus. *This extinct and undoubtedly savage marine predator reached a maximum length of 30 feet.*

Remains of a Pterodactyl (*or* Pterodactylus), *first discovered in 1784 in Germany by Italian naturalist Alessandro Collini. Cuvier later examined the specimen and declared it to be a flying reptile.*

to modern reptiles, Cuvier reasoned that it was a very ancient and extinct species. Not long afterward he examined a fossil reptile that had been recently unearthed in Germany. To Cuvier's surprise, the fossil showed the remains of wings, although it clearly was not a bird. He named it *Pterodactyl*, or "wing finger," and declared that it had been a flying reptile that had lived in the remote past and then become extinct.

Neither the *Mosasaurus* nor the *Pterodactyl* were dinosaurs, so Cuvier was not the first to identify and name a dinosaur. However, his pioneering work in the identification of ancient species opened the scientific debate about extinction. Of some 150 fossil species found in the basin of France's Seine River, Cuvier demonstrated, 90 no longer existed. His anatomic analyses were so complete and precise that many other scientists were compelled to agree with him, despite the fact that his view of extinction contradicted that of the Bible. He even sup-

plied what many saw as a convincing cause for periodic extinctions—natural catastrophes. Cuvier wrote:

> Living things without number were swept out of existence by the catastrophes. Those inhabiting the dry lands were engulfed by deluges [floods]. Others whose home was in the waters perished when the sea bottom suddenly became dry land; whole races were extinguished leaving mere traces of their existence, which are now difficult of recognition, even by the naturalist.

By showing that many animals, including large and exotic reptiles, had lived long ago and eventually died out, Cuvier laid the groundwork for the discovery of a special class of ancient reptiles—the dinosaurs.

A New Kind of Animal

After Cuvier's identification of *Mosasaurus* and *Pterodactyl*, searching for

Two long-necked plesiosaurs encounter a more massive Ichthyosaurus *in a warm Mesozoic lagoon. The diet of both ancient marine reptiles was primarily fish, although it is likely that adults of either species preyed upon young or wounded individuals of the other.*

remains of fossil reptiles became a popular pastime in Europe. Many amateur finds became famous, such as the discovery by a young English girl named Mary Anning of the skeleton of a thirty-foot-long marine monster. This creature later became known as *Ichthyosaurus*, or "fish lizard." But the distinction of first identifying what is now recognized as a dinosaur went to an English country doctor and amateur geologist named Gideon Mantell. According to the popular, but still unsubstantiated, story of the discovery, in 1822 Mantell's wife Mary found a large tooth poking out of a rock pile near a roadside and brought it to him. He supposedly said, "You have found the remains of an animal new to science."

Regardless of whether this account is factual, Mantell did subsequently discover more teeth and bones belonging to the same kind of animal. He concluded that they were extremely old but was at first at a complete loss to identify them. So he showed them to the two most eminent anatomists of the day—Cuvier in Paris, and William Buckland

in Oxford, England. Mantell told them that the fossils had come from very old layers of rocks, but the two experts were unsure of his analysis. They suggested that the relics were more recent and

Country doctor and naturalist Gideon Mantell (1790-1852). To his left are the femur bones of the huge Iguanodon *and the much smaller modern iguana lizard.*

Two lower teeth of an Iguanodon. *The newly formed, little-used tooth at left has sharp edges, while the other one has been worn down by constant chewing.*

iguana lizards, which are typically one to three feet long. The main difference was that his fossil teeth were much larger than those of iguanas. In 1825, Mantell published a description of what he called *Iguanodon*, or "iguana tooth." The beast, Mantell claimed, was an extinct land lizard that was about forty feet long and herbivorous, or plant eating. Cuvier quickly and graciously admitted his previous error and accepted Mantell's conclusions.

As it turned out, some of the details of Mantell's description of *Iguanodon* were incorrect. It was not, as he assumed, a direct ancestor of modern iguana lizards. He also wrongly envisioned the creature as walking on all fours like typical reptiles and thought its unusually large upright thumb bone was a horn that protruded from its head. Nevertheless, his estimate of the beast's size was essentially correct, as was his supposition that it was an herbivore. Most importantly, Mantell firmly established that large extinct reptiles

constituted the remains of a known creature, perhaps a large fish or a rhinoceros.

But Mantell stubbornly stuck to his original idea—that the fossils were those of a very ancient and probably extinct creature. After further research, he noticed that the teeth closely resembled those of living South American

In his initial reconstruction of Iguanodon, *Mantell mistakenly placed the beast's spikelike thumb, which he assumed was a horn, on the snout.*

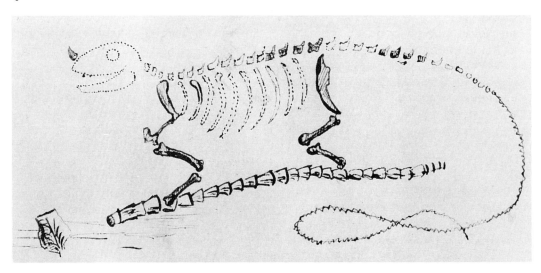

THE BIRTH OF DINOSAUR MANIA

On New Year's Eve in 1853, Richard Owen and Benjamin Waterhouse Hawkins threw a dinner party for twenty people inside their partially completed life-size model of Iguanodon.

The current public fascination for dinosaurs, exemplified by the enormous worldwide success of the 1993 film *Jurassic Park*, is not a new phenomenon. Earlier films, such as *King Kong* (1933), in which a giant ape battles various huge reptiles, similarly stimulated the public's interest in dinosaurs. Popular stories and novels—among them Sir Arthur Conan Doyle's *The Lost World* (1912), which featured adventurers discovering living dinosaurs on a remote plateau—did the same. However, these entertainments merely tapped into an existing dinosaur mania that actually began in England in 1854. The first world's fair, the 1851 Great Exhibition of the Works of Industry of All Nations, had recently closed in London. Engineers dismantled the fair's central building, a huge glass structure called the Crystal Palace, and reconstructed it in a park on the outskirts of the city. Those in charge of the project decided to decorate the grounds with full-size replicas of the giant reptiles discovered in recent decades. Richard Owen, the eminent scholar who had recently coined the term *dinosaur*, and well-known sculptor

Benjamin Waterhouse Hawkins, teamed up to create the models. These included reproductions of Mantell's *Iguanodon* and *Hylaeosaurus*, and Buckland's *Megalosaurus*, as well as several large extinct crocodiles and marine reptiles. Not much was known about dinosaurs at the time, so Owen and Hawkins made inadvertent anatomic mistakes. For instance, they depicted *Iguanodon* and *Megalosaurus* as standing on four legs. Scientists later learned that these beasts stood erect on their hind legs. But in the 1850s no one knew the difference, and the new exhibit was a success. Owen and Hawkins held a large dinner party inside the partially completed *Iguanodon* on New Year's Eve in 1853, and the exhibit opened soon afterward. Year after year, thousands of visitors flocked, as an observer of the time noted, "to witness the monsters that inhabited the earth before Noah." Dinosaurs had made a vivid and lasting impression on the public imagination. The huge models that gave birth to dinosaur mania still stand in London.

Some artifacts of early fossil hunting, among them a tiny jaw (under magnifying glass) given by William Buckland to Cuvier, and a book containing a drawing of Buckland (lower right).

had inhabited the land as well as the sea and air. He went on to discover another ancient land reptile in 1833. Called *Hylaeosaurus*, or "forest reptile," it was another herbivore, in this case with armor plating and large bony spines, like those of mythical dragons, running down its back.

In the meantime, William Buckland had identified his own extinct land reptile. In the mid-1820s, he described *Megalosaurus*, or "big reptile," as a carnivorous, or meat-eating, creature. After getting Cuvier's opinions about *Megalosaurus*'s large thighbone, Buckland wrote, "From these dimensions as compared with the ordinary standard of the lizard family, a length exceeding 40 feet and a bulk equal to that of an elephant seven feet high have been assigned by Cuvier to the individual to which this bone belonged."

Naming the Beasts

As more and more ancient reptiles and other prehistoric creatures were discovered, a whole new scientific field, one devoted to their study, came into being. In 1838, scientist Charles Lyell coined the term paleontology, Greek for "the science of ancient being," to describe the new field. Yet researchers still had not effectively named and categorized the kinds of creatures they were study-

This early drawing of Iguanodon *and* Megalosaurus *incorrectly depicts both as being quadrupeds, or four-legged animals. In reality, these creatures were bipeds that walked upright on two legs.*

ing. As late as 1840, for example, they continued to lump all extinct reptiles together, ignoring huge differences in anatomy and the fact that some lived on land and others in the sea.

This situation increasingly bothered the well-known English anatomist Richard Owen. He had closely studied the remains of *Iguanodon*, *Megalosaurus*, and *Hylaeosaurus* and had concluded that they showed significant differences from other ancient reptiles. First, Owen pointed out, these three creatures were land rather than sea dwellers. Second, they were huge—much larger than any known modern land reptiles. Third, and most important, their pelvic bones and bellies were raised from the ground so that they walked upright, more like mammals than lizards, which tend to drag themselves along the ground. These special creatures, Owen believed, should have their own separate classification. And in 1841 he invented one for them. He called them "dinosaurs," from the Greek words *deinos*, meaning "terrible," and *sauros*, meaning "lizard" or "reptile." Owen concluded:

> From the size and form of the ribs, it is evident that the trunk was broader and deeper in proportion than in modern

A portion of the lower jaw of the creature Buckland called Megalosaurus, *now known to be a theropod, a kind of bipedal meat-eating dinosaur.*

The teeth of Megalosaurus *and* Iguanodon *(top) rest on a book by Richard Owen (himself pictured below).*

> Saurians [lizards], and it was doubtless raised from the ground upon extremities [limbs] proportionally larger and especially longer, so that the general aspect of the living Megalosaur must have proportionally resembled that of the large [mammals] which now tread the earth, and the place [in nature] of which seems to have been supplied [in past ages] by the great reptiles of the extinct Dinosauria order.

In the year dinosaurs got their name, Cuvier had been dead for nine years, Mantell was fifty-one, and Buckland was fifty-seven. The old guard of fossil experts was passing, and Owen's colorful naming and descriptions of the "terrible lizards" captured the imagination of a new and eager generation of fossil hunters and adventurers. Under these researchers, the infant science of paleontology would experience a virtual explosion of new facts and findings. The first great age of dinosaur discovery was about to begin.

Bone Wars: The First Great Age of Discovery

For the study of dinosaurs, the first half of the nineteenth century had been a period of trial and error. Fossil hunters had made more or less random discoveries of ancient bones, and anatomists had then offered educated guesses about the creatures these specimens had once belonged to. By contrast, in the second half of the century the fledgling science of paleontology began to come into its own. Various museums, universities, governments, and private individuals funded numerous fossil-hunting expeditions and lengthy follow-up studies by scientists. This much larger, better-organized, and more systematic approach to finding and understanding dinosaur remains yielded thousands of new fossil specimens. It also vastly increased scientific knowledge about what dinosaurs were, how they lived, what the world was like when they roamed the earth, and how best to excavate and preserve their remains.

Public interest in dinosaurs profoundly affected the search for this knowledge. Thanks to Richard Owen's creation of life-size dinosaur models in a London park in the early 1850s and other similar exhibitions in museums, the public became fascinated by dinosaurs. The realization that giant monsters had actually once existed seemed to strike a chord with people from all walks of life. As public demand to see dinosaur remains steadily grew, scientists learned that they could gain both fame and money by discovering or exhibiting new dinosaurs. Many fossil hunters inevitably found themselves in competition. Some of this rivalry was friendly and honorable, but much of it was not.

Benjamin Waterhouse Hawkins's model of Iguanodon, *sculpted in 1853-1854 for display in a park outside of London. Note the incorrect features: four-legged stature and nose-horn.*

In the most infamous case, two eminent paleontologists openly and often ruthlessly attempted to advance their own careers and reputations at each other's expense. As they raced to outdo and discredit each other, the first great age of paleontological discovery became a virtual war over dinosaur bones.

The Power of Money

The two principal opponents in the bone wars of the nineteenth century were Othniel Charles Marsh, professor of paleontology at Yale University in Connecticut, and Edward Drinker Cope, an independent scientist based in Philadelphia. They and their decades-long feud were the driving forces behind most of the major dinosaur expeditions and discoveries of the age. And their story illustrates both the best and

Othniel Charles Marsh (1831-1899) was able to study dinosaurs at his leisure thanks to wealth inherited from a rich uncle.

Edward Drinker Cope (1840-1897), Marsh's archenemy, came from a Quaker family and possessed a brilliant, analytical mind.

the worst aspects of paleontology in that age. They and their various assistants and collectors found and named many new dinosaur species and significantly expanded knowledge of these creatures. In the process, they shifted the primary focus of dinosaur discovery and study from Europe to the United States. However, Cope's and Marsh's rivalry and greed for individual fame wasted much valuable time, effort, and resources. And their feud eventually contributed to a government cutback in research money that hurt the field of paleontology.

In fact, money had been the main tool Cope and Marsh had used to gain power and dominate American dinosaur research in the first place. Both were independently wealthy. Cope's father was a prosperous shipowner and Marsh inherited a fortune from his uncle, the rich financier George Peabody.

HOW FOSSILS FORM

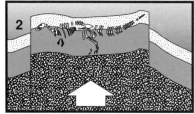

Originally, the term *fossil* referred to any artifact dug out of the ground. Today, it has a more specific meaning: the remains or preserved traces of an ancient living thing. One kind of fossil is an imprint left by an animal. For example, if a dinosaur walked through some soft mud and the mud had time to harden into stone before being washed away by rain, the fossil footprints might be preserved. Similarly, scientists have found imprint fossils of 530-million-year-old worms and jellyfish. Mud covered the creatures, hardened, and when the bodies decayed, detailed impressions of the bodies remained in the stone. Another kind of fossil forms when an animal dies and mud or other debris covers the body (1), forming a mold that eventually turns to rock. Inside the mold, protected from wind, rain, and sun, the soft parts of the body slowly decay, while water containing dissolved minerals seeps in. Over time, the minerals build up and harden and replace the bones, forming exact replicas. At the same time, the rock layer containing the fossil may shift so that it lies nearer the earth's surface (2). Millions of years later, wind, rain, or other natural forces might wear down the rock that encloses the fossilized skeleton, disclosing it to fortunate fossil hunters (3).

Cope's and Marsh's wealth allowed them to devote themselves full-time to paleontology and also to finance expeditions and to purchase specimens from various collectors. It also allowed them to outcompete and overshadow the careers of other equally talented but less well-to-do researchers.

The most eminent of these other researchers was Joseph Leidy, professor of anatomy at the University of Pennsylvania. Leidy made a name for himself in the 1850s and in the process initiated serious investigations of dinosaurs in the United States. Before that time, scientists had assumed that dinosaurs had inhabited mainly Europe and Asia. By showing that these ancient creatures had also roamed North America, Leidy opened the way for later spectacular fossil finds in the United States and Canada. In 1858, he examined some bones found in Montana and identified them as coming from a large, duck-billed, herbivorous dinosaur. He named the beast *Trachodon*, or "rough tooth." In the same year, Leidy declared that some fossil remains discovered in a Haddonfield, New Jersey, quarry belonged to another duck-billed herbivore, which he named *Hadrosaurus* after the town. Leidy later described *Hadrosaurus* as a "great herbivorous lizard [that] sustained itself in a semierect position on the huge hinder [rear] extremities and tail while it browsed on plants growing upon the shores of the ocean [near] which it lived."

For a few years, Leidy remained the most promising and respected paleontologist in the Americas. He served as director of the prestigious Academy of Natural Sciences in Philadelphia. As young men, both Cope and Marsh studied or worked with him. But as Cope and Marsh entered the field in earnest in the early 1870s, Leidy found that he could not effectively compete with them. As historian Ronald Rainger puts it:

Throughout the 1850s and 1860s Leidy had benefited from a system that provided him with specimens for free. Yet he was dependent on his network of underpaid collectors and not able to take full advantage of the [fossil] riches that lay in the West. Leidy was not a wealthy man and for much of his career maintained more than one job in order to make ends meet. Financial and teaching obligations did not permit Leidy to undertake expeditions independently, and he had no institutional support of his own.

By contrast, Cope and Marsh could afford to reward fossil collectors handsomely. Not surprisingly, as these collectors made increasingly more spectacular finds in the American West during the 1870s, they bypassed Leidy and sold them to Cope and Marsh. In a letter to a foreign colleague, a bitter Leidy wrote:

> Formerly, every fossil . . . found in the United States came to me, for nobody else cared to study such things, but

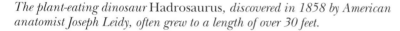

The plant-eating dinosaur Hadrosaurus, *discovered in 1858 by American anatomist Joseph Leidy, often grew to a length of over 30 feet.*

O.C. Marsh (back row, middle) and his colleagues pose before leaving for a hunting trip, perhaps for buffalo. The men donned similar outfits on their fossil-hunting expeditions.

Professors Marsh and Cope, with long purses, offer money for what used to come to me for nothing, and in that respect I cannot compete with them.

Thus, the first stage of the bone wars was the process by which Cope and Marsh used their wealth to overshadow their colleagues and establish themselves as the dominant figures in American paleontology.

The Race for Priority

The hatred and personal rivalry between Cope and Marsh constituted the second stage of the bone wars. The exact origins of this mutual hatred are difficult to trace. The two men had occasionally worked together in the 1860s, when they appeared to be on friendly terms. In 1867 Cope named a new species for Marsh and Marsh did the same for Cope two years later. In time, however, they started accusing each other of making errors in their descriptions and reconstructions of dinosaurs and other fossil beasts. The worst incident apparently occurred about 1870 when Cope showed Marsh a reconstructed skeleton of an *Elasmosaurus*, a large marine reptile. Marsh pointed out that Cope had mounted the head on the wrong end of the creature. According to their colleagues, the intensely proud and quick-tempered Cope flew into a rage and never forgave Marsh, who afterwards talked openly about Cope's error.

In the following decade, the disagreement erupted into open scientific warfare. Cope and Marsh sought constantly to establish priority over each other. In science, priority is the official recognition of having been the first to discover or invent something. In paleontology, the discoverer has the right to name a specimen, and his or her name is always associated with that find. To

Cope and Marsh, establishing priority was the main path to achieving prestige and bigger reputations. It also fed their egos. Historian James Secord explains, "Naming was an essential feature in this active process of achievement. To name something was to place it, to possess it."

In an attempt to gain priority, Cope and Marsh both poured large amounts of money into financing expeditions to the same areas. The three richest American dinosaur sites at the time were Bridger Basin and Como Bluff, both in Wyoming, and the Morrison formation near Canon City, Colorado. Como Bluff, where digging began in 1877, turned out to be the richest deposit of fossil dinosaurs ever discovered. Both men exploited these sites in a race to see who could find and name the most new species of dinosaurs. Typically, each also raced to be the first to publish his findings in scientific journals and thereby gain the all-important priority. Unfortunately, these hasty methods sometimes resulted in sloppy work that hindered the cause of science. According to biologist Stephen Jay Gould, as Cope and Marsh vied for glory

> they fell into a pattern of rush and superficiality born of their intense competition and mutual dislike. Both wanted to bag as many names as possible, so they published too quickly, often with inadequate descriptions, careless study, and poor illustrations. In this unseemly rush, they frequently gave names to fragmentary material that could not be well characterized [identified] and sometimes described the same creature twice by failing to make proper distinctions among the fragments.

These cross sections of the Como Bluff and Bone Cabin quarries in Wyoming show the rippled, or "folded," underground rock layers, among them the one containing dinosaur remains.

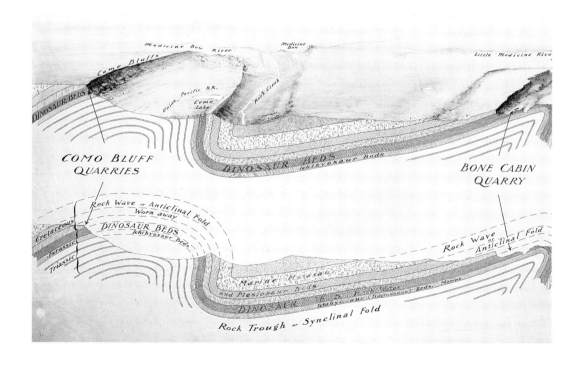

One of the best-known examples of erroneously describing the same animal twice was Marsh's naming of one of the most famous of all dinosaurs—*Brontosaurus*. In 1877, Marsh identified a new herbivorous dinosaur that he named *Apatosaurus*, a beast with a huge body, elephantlike legs, and a tiny head at the end of a long neck. Two years later Marsh described another set of remains as belonging to a related but different species. He called this one *Brontosaurus*, or "thunder lizard," presumably because it was so large the ground shook when it walked. But Marsh's analysis turned out to be incorrect. In the early 1900s scientists discovered that both sets of specimens were from the same kind of animal. Because the name *Apatosaurus* had come first, the beast thereafter officially bore that name. But it was already too late for the public. Huge skeletons in museums, as well as pictures in magazines and books, had for years borne the name of *Brontosaurus*. And this was the name that stuck in the popular media, thanks to Marsh's haste.

Dirty Tactics

Scientific errors were not the only negative aspect of the Cope-Marsh feud. Both men regularly attacked each other in scientific publications and newspaper articles. For instance, Marsh publicly accused Cope of attempting to gain priority illegally by predating, or claiming to have found specimens before he really did. The two men also carried their dirty tactics into the field, or the sites where fossils were dug up. Each employed spies to find out what the other's workers were doing. According to some accounts, they also used money to lure away each other's workers and on occasion even hired thugs to destroy each other's specimens.

In the 1880s and 1890s, the bone wars entered a third phase. During these years, both Cope and Marsh depleted most of their personal fortunes by unwise spending and investments. They, along with younger scientists who had trained under them, tried to gain control of all available funding. The

This modern depiction of Apatosaurus (or Brontosaurus) *shows the correct elevated position of the tail. Earlier reconstructions mistakenly showed the beast dragging its tail along the ground.*

biggest prize was money allocated by the U.S. Congress for scientific research. Each scientist sought to get more money for himself by discrediting the others. Partly because of Marsh's influence with government officials, Cope repeatedly tried but failed to get government backing. Marsh enjoyed federal money for a while, but attacks by Cope and other colleagues prompted a congressional investigation that found many of his projects "worthless." Marsh lost his funding and had to suspend his field research. The unfortunate result of all this turmoil was that the volume of paleontological expeditions and research decreased in the 1890s.

To their credit, in spite of their destructive feud, Cope and Marsh significantly advanced knowledge about dinosaurs. Between them they found or identified 136 new dinosaur species. Among these were *Camarasaurus* and *Diplodocus*, huge lumbering plant eaters like *Apatosaurus*; the carnivorous *Allosaurus*, a savage hunter standing more than fifteen feet high with a mouthful

The skull of Diplodocus, *an herbivorous giant measuring almost 90 feet in length and weighing 10-11 tons.*

of daggerlike teeth; *Stegosaurus*, a squat herbivore with huge bony plates running down its back; and *Triceratops*, or "three-horned face," a rhinolike grazing monster built like an army tank.

Developing Field Methods

Cope, Marsh, and their colleagues also developed or refined field methods of dating and preserving fossil specimens.

The huge theropod meat eater Allosaurus, *first discovered in Colorado in 1869, lived during the Jurassic period. An adult specimen of this vicious hunting species had a skull 2-3 feet long and a body length of 30-40 feet.*

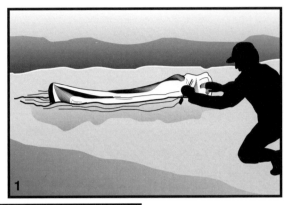

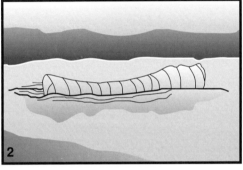

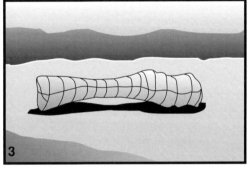

The traditional method scientists use to remove and preserve large fossil bones is: (1) to dig away the soil, exposing one-half or more of the bone, (2) to pack wet paper or aluminum foil around the exposed area, then cover it with plaster of paris or polyurethane foam to provide a protective coating, and (3) to remove the rest of the bone, turn it over, and apply the same casing to the remaining exposed surface. The preserved bone can now be safely transported to a museum lab.

They had no inkling of the real age of the earth—about 4.6 billion years; the oldest estimate of the time was a mere 100 million years. So they could not accurately date their finds. They did, however, use and improve on a method pioneered in the late 1700s called comparative, or relative, dating. Researchers observed the way rocks beneath the earth's surface are laid down in layers called strata. The deeper the stratum, the older it is, so fossil remains found in a particular stratum are obviously older than those in the stratum above and younger than those in the stratum below. Thus, dinosaurs found in one stratum are clearly either older or younger than those in other strata. Comparative dating showed Cope, Marsh, and other scientists which creatures developed

In this museum reconstruction, Albertosaurus, *a smaller but still lethal relative of* T-rex, *stands over its kill—* Centrosaurus, *a horned plant eater related to* Triceratops.

first and which lived and coexisted in the same period.

Many of the bone preservation techniques developed by Cope, Marsh, and their assistants are still in use today. To protect the fragile fossils during transport to museum laboratories, Cope's workers wrapped the specimens in casts. They made the casts by boiling rice into a thick paste, dipping burlap strips into the paste, and then wrapping them around the bones and letting them harden. Marsh's men used flour paste and strong paper to achieve the same effect. Another method was to improvise bandages of cloth and plaster of paris to make casts.

Scientists in other countries adopted these basic but effective preservation methods developed by American dinosaur hunters. However, during the period of the bone wars, few significant dinosaur finds occurred outside of the United States. The most spectacular was in 1878 in Bernissart, Belgium, where coal miners uncovered some forty complete or partial *Iguanodon* skeletons. After studying and mounting the bones, European researchers confirmed that Owen and other early experts had been wrong in describing the creature as walking on all fours. *Iguanodon* was instead a biped, an animal that walks upright on two legs. Another important discovery was that of the skull of *Albertosaurus*, a large carnivorous hunting dinosaur, in Alberta, Canada, in 1884. This find was especially important because it foreshadowed a major Canadian dinosaur rush in the early years of the next century. In fact, the next great age of dinosaur discovery would witness major finds on almost every continent, confirming that these ancient beasts had ruled not simply a few areas, but the entire globe.

Desert Quest: Creatures of the Flaming Cliffs

The destructive bitterness and waste of the bone wars of the late 1800s taught most American paleontologists a valuable lesson. Although they remained ambitious and competitive, they thereafter refrained from actively undermining each other's work. And most learned to cooperate for the overall betterment of science. They also worked at a less hurried pace, were more cautious and methodical, and therefore made fewer mistakes. As the twentieth century dawned, a more disciplined group of dinosaur hunters set the standard of professionalism that has characterized the field ever since.

Some of these researchers continued to work at Como Bluff and other known and still rich U.S. fossil deposits. Others gained fame and success by dis-

covering new dinosaur sites. In 1909 Earl Douglass of Pittsburgh's Carnegie Museum found the richest new site near Vernal, Utah, which yielded numerous skeletons of *Apatosaurus*, *Diplodocus*, *Stegosaurus*, *Allosaurus*, and many other dinosaurs. In 1915 President Woodrow Wilson gave this impressive site the name it still bears: Dinosaur National Monument.

Dinosaurs Around the World

Despite continued rich American finds, however, the United States no longer dominated the field of paleontology. In this new age of discovery, which spanned the first three decades of the

Split Mountain and Green River highlight this section of Dinosaur National Monument near Vernal, Utah, a site discovered in 1909.

twentieth century, dinosaur remains were discovered in many other parts of the world. These finds not only showed conclusively that dinosaurs existed all over the earth, but also indicated that all dinosaurs lived during one specific era, the Mesozoic. No matter which country or continent dinosaur specimens came from, researchers always found them in specific rock strata. These were the layers associated with the three Mesozoic periods: the Triassic, Jurassic, and Cretaceous. Remains of *Plateosaurus*, a large herbivore, always came from Triassic strata; those of *Allosaurus*, from Jurassic strata; and those of *Triceratops*, from Cretaceous strata. This showed that various dinosaur species periodically became extinct, giving way to new species. The evidence also clearly indicated that, for reasons unknown, all dinosaurs became extinct at the end of the Cretaceous period.

In the first few years of the twentieth century, scientists still did not know the actual ages of the Mesozoic strata. So they could not accurately date dinosaur remains or tell exactly when all dinosaurs became extinct. The situation improved somewhat between 1905 and 1910, when researchers began using absolute dating in conjunction with comparative dating. In absolute dating, scientists date strata directly by measuring the amounts and proportions of radioactive elements present in the rocks. At the time, this method rendered estimates of about 2 billion years for the age of the earth and at least 100 million years for the beginning of the Mesozoic era. Later refinements in the technique showed that these estimates were still too conservative. But they were some twenty times more accurate than the guesses made a mere decade before

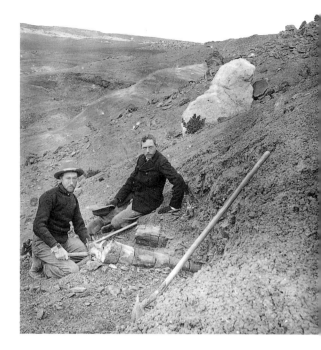

American excavator Barnum Brown (left) with Henry F. Osborn, both of the American Museum of Natural History, at the Como Bluff dig in the early 1900s.

and certainly a far cry from Bishop Ussher's calculations.

Absolute dating became a standard tool of the fossil hunters who explored several remote regions of the world between 1907 and 1930. Some of the best-known and most exciting finds occurred in Canada. Between 1910 and 1916, Barnum Brown, of New York's American Museum of Natural History, unearthed numerous dinosaur specimens along the Red Deer River in central Alberta. Among these were nearly complete skeletons of *Monoclonius*, a relative of *Triceratops* bearing one horn instead of three, and *Corythosaurus*, a duck-billed herbivore. Canadian researchers led by Charles H. Sternberg soon launched their own expedition to the area and discovered many new

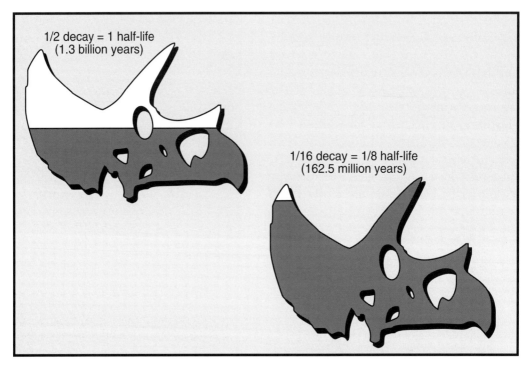

1/2 decay = 1 half-life
(1.3 billion years)

1/16 decay = 1/8 half-life
(162.5 million years)

The technique of absolute dating uses radioactive isotopes, unstable forms of certain elements. The atoms of an isotope slowly give off microscopic particles, a process known as radioactive decay. Over time, the atoms change into a stable, or unchanging, form of another element. The amount of time it takes for half of a given sample of an element to decay is that element's *half-life*. By measuring the amount of the isotope left in the sample, scientists can estimate how long decay has been occurring, and thus, the age of the sample. For example, the isotope carbon 14 has a half-life of 5,700 years. Suppose that an ancient piece of wood contains one-quarter the normal amount of carbon 14 found in a living tree. Half of the carbon 14 in the sample decayed in 5,700 years and half of what was left, or another quarter, decayed in another 5,700 years. This left the quarter still detectable in the sample. So a reliable estimate for the age of the wood is 5,700 + 5,700, or about 11,400 years. The half-life of carbon 14 is much too small to measure the great ages of rocks and fossils from the Mesozoic era or before. For this task scientists usually use the isotope potassium 40, which has a half-life of 1.3 billion years. After 1.3 billion years have passed, one-half of the potassium 40 in a fossil will have decayed. Consider a dinosaur fossil found in hardened lava in which $\frac{1}{16}$ of the potassium 40 has decayed. This is the same as saying that $\frac{1}{8}$ of half of the potassium 40 has decayed. Dividing potassium 40's half-life of 1.3 billion years by 8 produces a figure of 162.5 million years, dating the fossil to the middle of the Jurassic period.

dinosaur species. German excavators found new dinosaurs in what is now Tanzania in eastern Africa between 1907 and 1912. And between 1915 and 1930, Russian, Swedish, French, and Chinese researchers explored dinosaur sites in northern China.

By far the most famous and spectacular expedition of the age, however, was an American venture into Mongolia's desolate Gobi Desert in the 1920s. This expedition yielded some of the most exciting dinosaur discoveries ever. It also captured the public imagination and came to symbolize the air of adventure and mystery that surrounded dinosaur hunting at the time.

Fulfilling a Lifelong Dream

The great Gobi expedition was organized and led by a Wisconsin naturalist and adventurer named Roy Chapman Andrews. Exploring the wonders of nature had been his lifelong dream, beginning in early childhood. In his 1929 book *Ends of the Earth*, he wrote, "Nothing else ever had a place in my mind. Every moment that I could steal from school was spent in the woods. . . . To enter the American Museum of Natural History was my life ambition." Filled with determination, Andrews did whatever was necessary to fulfill that

Barnum Brown (left) inspects a reconstructed skeleton of Triceratops, *or "three-horned face." The upper horns, nearly as long as the men, must have been formidable when used for defense.*

Roy Chapman Andrews (right) and an assistant contemplate a nest containing a dozen dinosaur eggs in the desert wasteland near Shabarakh Usu, Mongolia.

ambition. According to science writer Don Lessem, he

> wangled a job sweeping floors and working in the museum's taxidermy department [where animals were stuffed and mounted] when he was fresh out of college and didn't leave the museum's employ for decades. Within a few years of joining the museum, he'd explored the wild forests of Korea, searched for a reported blue tiger in southern China, hunted whales off the coasts of Alaska and Japan, and spied for the Allies in China in World War I.

After the war, Andrews began approaching wealthy individuals to finance a proposed expedition to Mongolia. At this stage, dinosaurs were the furthest thing from his mind, his goal being to find traces of early humans. American Museum president Henry Fairfield Osborn had earlier suggested that humans originated in central Asia. Inspired by this idea, Andrews reasoned that the Gobi Desert, where shifting sands commonly expose ancient rock strata, would be an ideal place to search for human fossils.

Having obtained the necessary funding, Andrews arrived in Peking, China, in 1921 and began organizing the expedition. His plan, an unusual innovation at the time, was to use automobiles rather than the usual camel caravan to traverse the immense arid desert wastes. This approach, he reasoned, would allow his team to explore ten times the area that a slow-moving camel caravan could in a single season. While waiting for the autos to be shipped from the United States, Andrews assembled his team. The group included two geologists, a physician, a photographer, and the respected paleontologist Walter Granger, as well as mechanics, cooks, and helpers.

On April 21, 1922, the expedition departed China and entered the Gobi. Andrews had wisely sent a camel caravan ahead to plant piles of gasoline, oil, and foodstuffs at strategic points along the planned route. This left the autos free to carry tents, digging tools, water, and of course the members of the expedition. After traveling about 250 miles in four days, the team reached a bleak expanse of salt marshes and sand mounds known as Iren Dabasu. The men camped there for the night. The next morning they began exploring the area and immediately found fossils, although these were of a decidedly different nature than expected. As John Wilford tells it, one man found part of a leg bone and

> to Granger it appeared reptilian. Presently, Granger walked up to the crest of the ridge and fell to his knees. He began brushing the sand away from something embedded in the ground. It was the tibia [lower leg bone] of a large reptile. Any doubt that Granger might have harbored was now dispelled. This was the bone of a dinosaur, the first known in Mongolia and one of the first known anywhere in eastern Asia.

Littered with Fossils

For Andrews and his colleagues, the discovery that the Gobi held dinosaur remains was as thrilling as it was unexpected. Eager with anticipation, the team pressed on into the desert and in mid-May made another important find. It consisted of teeth belonging to a *Baluchitherium*, an extinct rhinoceros. The largest land mammal that ever existed, it evolved long after the dinosaurs had become extinct. The explorers were certainly happy at this discovery, but their earlier find had infected them with a kind of dinosaur fever and they hoped their quest would uncover more dinosaurs.

The men soon found that hope fulfilled beyond their wildest dreams. Heading toward China on the return leg of their journey, they came to a large basin lined with vertical walls of red sandstone. Awed by the way the setting sun made the stone look like glowing embers, the explorers named them the "Flaming Cliffs." Even more awesome was their realization that the area was literally littered with fossil bones. Andrews later wrote:

> From our tents, we looked down into a vast pink basin, studded with giant buttes [rock towers] like strange beasts,

The auto caravan of Andrews's historic "Central Asiatic Expedition of the American Museum of Natural History" enters the Gobi Desert.

carved from sandstone. One of them we named the "dinosaur," for it resembles a huge *Brontosaurus* sitting on its haunches. There appear to be medieval castles with spires and turrets, brick-red in the evening light, colossal gateways, walls and ramparts. Caverns run deep into the rock and a labyrinth [maze] of ravines and gorges studded with fossil bones makes a paradise for the paleontologist.

The excited team members combed the area and returned to camp with armloads of fossils, most of which they had found on or near the surface of the ground.

Unfortunately, the men could not stay to explore the area further. The cold Mongolian winter was setting in fast, and they had to make it back to China as quickly as possible. Reluctantly, they departed the Flaming Cliffs and reached Peking in September. Andrews immediately sent one of his men to New York with one of the best-preserved of the newly found fossils, a reptilian skull. After examining the find, the enthusiastic Henry Osborn cabled Andrews: "You have made a very important discovery. The reptile is the long-sought ancestor of *Triceratops*. It has been named *Proto-*

ceratops andrewsi in your honor. Go back and get more." This urging was completely unnecessary, for the adventurous Andrews was already in the midst of planning the next trip into the Gobi.

Finding Wondrous Treasures

The second expedition departed in April 1923. This time the explorers found unusual dangers in their path. On their way to Iren Dabasu, the site of their first dinosaur finds the year before, mounted bandits attacked them. The quick-thinking and daring Andrews drove his car directly at the bandits, who fled when their horses panicked. Thanks to a military escort provided by the Mongolian government, the expedition managed to avoid further attacks.

After reaching Iren Dabasu, the team camped and quickly began searching for fossils. The site proved extremely rich in dinosaur specimens. Though this time the team members stayed for a full month and also had the benefit of three more fossil collectors assigned by Osborn, they barely began

The "Flaming Cliffs," a basin lined with vertical walls of red sandstone, where Andrews and his men found large concentrations of dinosaur fossils.

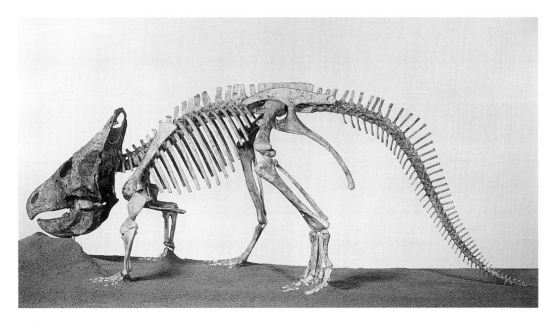

A skeleton of Protoceratops, *a small, hornless ancestor of horned plant-eating dinosaurs such as* Triceratops, Monoclonius, Centrosaurus, *and* Pentaceratops, *or "five-horned face."*

to exploit the potential of the site. At the end of May, the men left the area, having unearthed the remains of several meat- and plant-eating dinosaurs.

After more traveling and exploring, the expedition arrived at its primary destination—the Flaming Cliffs—in early July. The five-week stay at the site yielded a vast and wondrous collection of fossil treasures. Among these were seventy skulls and fourteen skeletons belonging to *Protoceratops*. As Osborn had suggested, this was the hornless ancestor of the ceratopsians, or horned dinosaurs, such as *Triceratops* and *Monoclonius*. The most exciting find at the site consisted of dinosaur eggs and nests, the first ever discovered. Andrews and his colleagues believed these had belonged to *Protoceratops*. After studying the eggs, some of which still bore tiny skeletons, and also the shape and placement of the nests, the men theorized

about how dinosaurs had laid their eggs. Evidently, the mothers had dug pits in the mud, laid the eggs in circles within the pits, and then covered them with a thin layer of sand. For reasons unknown, these particular eggs had never hatched, and the mud, sand, and eggs had turned to stone over time.

Robber Dinosaurs

The expedition made other important discoveries at the Flaming Cliffs. Among them were the remains of two small but lethal carnivorous dinosaurs that might have died in the act of robbing the *Protoceratops* nests. Scientists subsequently dubbed these creatures *Oviraptor*, or "egg stealer," and *Velociraptor*, or "fast-running robber." The men also found a skull belonging to a small ratlike mammal. Only one other mammal skull had

A nest of Protoceratops *eggs discovered by Roy Chapman Andrews during one of his expeditions to the Gobi Desert.*

been found previously in Mesozoic strata, and scientists had been unsure of whether mammals had developed that early. This new skull seemed to confirm that mammals had indeed shared the Mesozoic era with dinosaurs.

When the explorers returned to Peking late in 1923, they found that the news of their discoveries, especially of the eggs, had created a worldwide media sensation. Andrews, now a house-hold name in the United States and Europe, had no trouble raising the money for more trips into the Gobi. Three more expeditions, in 1925, 1928, and 1930, yielded more dinosaur bones and eggs and several more mammal skulls.

Andrews and other collectors wanted to continue exploring the Gobi's fossil treasures. But after 1930 they found politics a more powerful force than scientific curiosity. In Mongolia, China, and other parts of Asia, local officials had become hostile to foreigners "robbing priceless artifacts" from Asians. So mounting major expeditions into the area was now too difficult and dangerous. In fact, the situation for fossil hunters had become bleak everywhere and would remain so for a long time. The severe economic depression that swept the world in the 1930s was followed by the global conflict of World War II, and it became nearly impossible to raise funds for nonessential projects such as dinosaur research.

Andrews also discovered several remains of Oviraptor, *or "egg stealer," in the Gobi. This slender creature was about 5 feet long and had a toothless jaw with which it bit and crushed eggshells.*

In this reconstructed scene from the ancient Gobi, a pack of Velociraptors, *small carnivorous hunters measuring about 5-6 feet from snout to tail tip, launch a coordinated attack on a lone* Protoceratops.

Thus, the great era of large-scale and adventurous fossil exploration that had begun with the bone wars in the 1860s drew to a close. The result was a major change in the nature of paleontological work. John Wilford explains:

> The practice of making broad, sweeping reconnaissance expeditions gave way . . . to fieldwork of a more narrow scope: digging in one small area, examining in depth one period of geologic time, searching not so much for new species of dinosaurs as for a better understanding of the lives and times of the dinosaurs whose bones had already been [found].

Old-style adventurers like Andrews largely found themselves frustrated in desk jobs for the rest of their days. But Andrews himself managed to turn his captivity at a desk to the lasting benefit of science. He penned twenty-two books, all of them exciting yarns about the romance of digging up dinosaurs and other ancient beasts. These writings not only entertained millions, but also profoundly inspired a whole new generation of dinosaur hunters.

Terrible Claw: A Cold Look at Warm Blood

The period between 1930 and the mid-1960s witnessed a relative lull in dinosaur hunting. Scientists still studied, theorized on, and wrote about these ancient beasts. And small-scale excavations went on periodically at established fossil sites in the United States, Canada, and other areas around the world. But the old-fashioned, large-scale fieldwork that had emphasized exploring for, collecting, and naming new species was largely a thing of the past. When the study of dinosaurs underwent a kind of rebirth in the 1960s and 1970s, the emphasis was different. Scientists now seemed less interested in collecting and displaying dinosaurs and more interested in discovering what made the creatures tick. Researchers began to rethink old ideas about how dinosaurs lived, their hunting and reproductive habits, their physical attributes, and the reasons for their extinction. New studies of old specimens, as well as some evidence from new finds, resulted in dramatic changed, or revisionist, theories that challenged the old assumptions.

In a sense, one well-known scientist's work bridged the gap between the old paleontology and the new. He was Edwin H. Colbert, who as a young man studied with Henry Osborn and then went on to do small-scale but important fieldwork in the 1940s and 1950s. Colbert, called by *Time* magazine "The Dick Tracy of the Mesozoic Age," single-handedly discovered more than fifty new dinosaur species.

Some of Colbert's observations and ideas foreshadowed later revisionist concepts. Particularly important in this respect was Colbert's 1947 discovery of

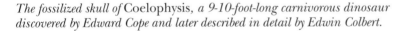

The fossilized skull of Coelophysis, *a 9-10-foot-long carnivorous dinosaur discovered by Edward Cope and later described in detail by Edwin Colbert.*

A Coelophysis *herd moves through a moist Triassic landscape. Scientists believe that such bipedal dinosaurs bobbed their heads, as birds do, as they walked along.*

several nearly complete skeletons of *Coelophysis.* This was a bipedal carnivorous dinosaur originally described by Edward Cope from just a few fossil fragments. Compared with the most famous meat-eating bipeds, such as *Allosaurus*—thirty-nine feet from nose to tail tip—and the even larger *Tyrannosaurus rex,* or *T. rex, Coelophysis* was tiny. Colbert noted that the smaller carnivore—only nine feet from nose to tail tip—had long, birdlike legs. These limbs seemed to be designed for fast running, perhaps, Colbert reasoned, in pursuit of prey. But the idea of a fast, active dinosaur was at odds with accepted theories about dinosaur structure and behavior. Colbert found himself wrestling with a question that would later spark the first of the revisionist debates: were the dinosaurs cold- or warm-blooded?

Overgrown Alligators and Lizards?

Like other paleontologists before him, Colbert had always assumed that dinosaurs were cold-blooded like other reptiles. Cold-blooded animals are unable to control their body temperatures, and their blood and tissues get warmer or cooler with their surroundings. Modern reptiles, for example, bask in the sun to build up warmth and energy. Yet even warmed-up reptiles have little energy and are slow moving. As scientist Robert Bakker explains:

> Generally, paleontologists have assumed that in everyday details of life, dinosaurs were merely overgrown alligators or lizards. Crocodilians and lizards spend much of their time in inactivity,

GALLOPING DINOS?

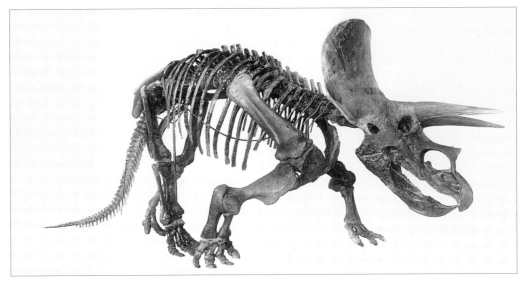

Prominent in this Triceratops *skeleton are the massive leg bones that may have helped give the beast the ability to gallop, despite its enormous bulk.*

Paleontologist Robert Bakker has been an unflinching supporter of the warm-blooded dinosaur hypothesis. He has argued that the heightened activity levels, low predator-to-prey ratios, and relatively large brains of some dinosaurs were more characteristic of warm-blooded than of cold-blooded creatures. He also maintains that having warm blood allowed many large dinosaurs to run as fast as today's large mammals. As evidence, he cites dinosaurs' upright posture, forward gait, and strong and flexible leg joints. In *The Dinosaur Heresies*, Bakker offers the following view of galloping dinosaurs, one many opponents of the warm-blooded idea consider largely fanciful:

> How fast might the big dinosaurs have been? Most twentieth-century paleontologists had been willing to concede lively locomotion to the . . . smaller predators, but the big two-ton-plus species were always reconstructed as slow shufflers. But large mammals can gallop. While in South Africa I observed three-ton white rhino bulls at a full gallop with all four huge feet off the ground simultaneously in mid-stride. . . . Perhaps big quadrupedal [four-legged] dinosaurs could also quick-start off into their own clomping high-speed charge. . . . The biggest meat-eater, three-ton-plus *Tyrannosaurus* [a biped] . . . could easily have over-hauled a galloping white rhino—at speeds above forty miles per hour, for sure. . . . *Triceratops* [a quadruped] had tremendously strong limb bones, and that strength must have evolved to withstand great forces. The un-believers who scoff at the notion of a galloping *Triceratops* will have to explain why dinosaurs evolved such strong, thickly shafted limbs if they were going to do no exercise more strenuous than a shuffle through the swamps.

sunning themselves on a convenient rock or log, and . . . most modern reptiles are slow and sluggish. Hence the usual reconstruction of a dinosaur such as *Brontosaurus* is a mountain of scaly flesh which moved around only slowly and infrequently.

Similarly, scientists saw dinosaur predators, or hunters, as incapable of great exertion or activity. Prevailing opinion envisioned the giant *T. rex* waiting in ambush to jump out at its prey rather than chasing after it.

It seemed to Colbert that *Coelophysis* did not fit into this standard view of sluggish dinosaurs. In fact, the evidence suggested that the small biped behaved more like a warm-blooded animal. Creatures with warm blood, such as mammals and birds, maintain a nearly constant and relatively warm body temperature, giving them a ready supply of energy on which to draw. They also have highly efficient hearts that can pump more blood faster than the hearts of reptiles. For these reasons, warm-blooded animals are quite active.

Not yet ready to accept the idea of warm-blooded dinosaurs, Colbert searched for an alternate explanation for *Coelophysis*'s apparent high activity levels. To learn more about how reptiles retain warmth, he carefully studied the body temperatures of modern alligators. He placed specimens of various sizes in the sun until they were very warm, then measured their temperatures at intervals as they cooled down. Colbert found that the larger the gator, the slower it cooled down. This suggested that bigger body mass could retain heat longer. The fact that most dinosaurs had a great deal of body mass, Colbert reasoned, might explain how they could be cold-blooded and at least

in some instances behave in a warm-blooded fashion.

Decidedly Unreptilian Behavior

Scientists continued to accept dinosaur cold-bloodedness without question until 1964. In August of that year, a Yale University paleontologist named John Ostrom and his assistant, Grant E. Meyer, made a startling discovery that forever changed the way people saw dinosaurs.

Paleontologist John Ostrom holds the "terrible" claw of Deinonychus, *the small but savage hunter he discovered in 1964.*

Deinonychus *probably used its backwardly curved teeth, plainly visible in this view of the creature's skull, to tear chunks of meat off of its unfortunate prey.*

One day, while searching for Cretaceous fossils near Bridger, Montana, they spotted what appeared to be a claw at the bottom of a sloping mound. Ostrom later recalled, "We both nearly rolled down the slope in our rush to the spot. In front of us, clearly recognizable, was a good portion of a large-clawed hand protruding from the surface."

After some feverish digging, the two men excavated the three-fingered claw and also some sharp teeth, all of these from an unknown carnivore. Next came the most amazing find: the perfectly preserved bones of the creature's foot. To Ostrom's surprise, it was radically different from any known dinosaur foot. Instead of having three clawed toes, with the middle one slightly longer than the other two, this beast had two outer toes about the same length. The inner toe bore a very long, curved, and bony claw shaped like a sickle blade. So Ostrom named the creature *Deinonychus* meaning "terrible claw."

This highly unusual foot made Ostrom start thinking about dinosaur warm-bloodedness. Having studied under Edwin Colbert, he was familiar with Colbert's observations of *Coelophysis* and the supposition that it was a fast-moving, active creature. *Deinonychus*, Ostrom reasoned, must have been active, too. "Common sense tells us," he wrote, "that a sharp, thin, recurved sickle-like blade is for cutting or slashing and not for digging, tree-climbing or providing traction on the ground." *Deinonychus*, he declared, was a biped that chased down and used its hind feet to slash its prey. But this is decidedly unreptilian behavior. "It does not surprise us," Ostrom went on,

> to see an eagle or hawk slash with its talons, or stand on one foot and lash out with the other. But to imagine a lizard or a crocodile—or any modern reptile—standing on its hind legs and attacking is ridiculous. Reptiles are just not capable of such intricate maneuvers, such delicate balance, poise, and agility—such demanding activity.

Ostrom was not suggesting that *Deinonychus* was not a reptile. Like all other dinosaurs, it clearly was. But it was one reptile that clearly behaved in a warm-blooded manner. Ostrom was not satisfied with the explanation of such behavior advanced by Colbert for *Coelophysis*—namely, large body mass temporarily retaining warmth to fuel heightened activity. *Deinonychus* was a slender, lightly built creature with very little body mass. An adult stood only six feet tall and weighed just 150 to 175 pounds. Ostrom thought that it could not have retained the warmth it needed to hunt and attack the way it obviously did through body mass alone. Ostrom's argument seemed to suggest that dinosaurs, or at least the predators, might have been a special, warm-blooded kind of reptile. He wrote in a scientific journal:

> The foot of *Deinonychus* is perhaps the most revealing bit of anatomical evidence pertaining to dinosaurian habits and [the *Deinonychus*] must have been anything but "reptilian" in its behavior, responses, and way of life. It must have been a fleet-footed, highly predaceous [stalking and hunting], extremely agile and very active animal, sensitive to many stimuli and quick in its responses. These in turn indicate an unusual level of activity for a reptile and suggest an unusually high metabolic [energy-producing] rate. . . . There is considerable evidence, which is impressive, if not compelling, that many different kinds of ancient reptiles were characterized by mammalian or avian [bird] levels of metabolism.

Debate Continues

Ostrom's tentative conclusions about *Deinonychus* ignited a fervent debate among paleontologists, one that has continued to the present. Some of his colleagues saw merit in the idea of warm-blooded dinosaurs, saying that it

This modern drawing shows how Deinonychus *probably held its sicklelike claw upright to use as an effective slashing tool when attacking its prey.*

explained much about dinosaur behavior. Others remained skeptical, insisting that the evidence was still weak. Among the supporting evidence was the fact that dinosaur bones contain haversian tissue, a dense network of microscopic blood vessels usually seen only in large mammals. This seemed to suggest that dinosaurs had circulatory systems similar to those of warm-blooded creatures. Opponents countered by pointing out that some modern turtles and crocodiles, which are clearly cold-blooded, have haversian bone tissue. Such tissue, they said, might be related more to rapid growth rates than to warm-bloodedness.

Ostrom and his supporters offered other evidence for warm-blooded dinosaurs. They suggested that the erect posture exhibited by bipedal dinosaurs, many of them carnivores like *Deinonychus*, is more characteristic of mammals than reptiles. Ostrom also maintained that the vertical distance between the hearts and brains of many dinosaurs was relatively large. The greater the heart-brain distance in an animal, the harder the heart must pump to push blood to the brain and hence the higher the blood pressure. For that reason, a giraffe's blood pressure is twice as high as that of a human. To maintain their high blood pressure, Ostrom argued, dinosaurs probably had efficient, four-chambered hearts, a feature normally seen only in warm-blooded animals. Ostrom's opponents rejected this idea. They maintained that since no dinosaurian soft tissue, including hearts, has survived for examination, any description of such tissue is mere guesswork.

As the debate raged on into the 1970s, Robert Bakker, an outspoken pa-leontologist who had once been one of Ostrom's students, championed the warm blood hypothesis. Bakker said that dinosaur predator-prey relationships proved these beasts were warm-blooded. Because warm-blooded creatures burn food faster, they must eat more often than reptiles. This means that warm-blooded predators such as lions need a much larger supply of food. To ensure survival, such predators maintain much smaller populations than their prey, as evidenced by the example of African predators, which make up only about 4 percent of the continent's overall animal population. Bakker proposed counting specimens

Robert Bakker, the controversial paleontologist who strongly advocated in his 1986 book, The Dinosaur Heresies, *that dinosaurs were warm-blooded.*

PREDATOR-PREY RATIOS

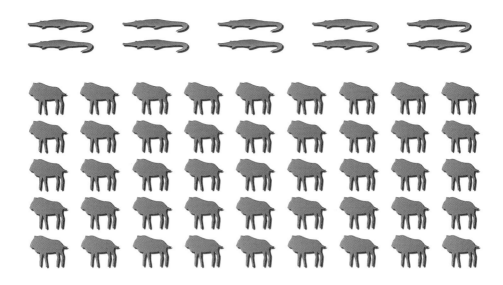

According to modern research, one warm-blooded lion consumes as much food as about ten cold-blooded crocodiles. That means that lions' prey need to be about ten times more numerous than crocodiles' prey, resulting in a higher predator-prey ratio for warm-blooded creatures such as lions. If it can be proven that dinosaurs had high predator-prey ratios, it might suggest that dinosaurs were warm-blooded. However, the exact nature of predator-prey ratios among dinosaurs remains unclear.

of predators such as the allosaurs—the family that included the carnivorous *Allosaurus.* "To determine the allosaurs' metabolism," Bakker explained in his controversial book, *The Dinosaur Heresies,*

> all that was required was a count of the number of specimens and a comparison with the number of prey specimens found in the same strata. If allosaurs were always rare compared to all their prey, as rare as lions are relative to zebra and antelope, it would provide direct evidence that the predatory dinosaurs needed a very large weekly ration of meat.

No Consensus

According to Bakker's count, predatory dinosaurs constituted about 2 percent of the overall dinosaur population. This, he proposed, indicated that these predators hunted and ate often and were therefore active, warm-blooded creatures. Bakker forcefully presented this argument in 1978 at the annual meeting of the American Association for the Advancement of Science in Washington, D.C. Most of his colleagues criticized his findings, however. They held that it was

A graphic depiction of predator and prey: an Allosaurus *attacks a juvenile* Diplodocus. *It is unlikely that the larger beast will escape.*

impossible for Bakker to get an accurate count of the dinosaurs that lived in a given area simply by counting fossils. They argued that fossilization is a rare and random process. Perhaps by chance more of the prey than the predators in the area became fossilized, giving the false impression that prey greatly outnumbered predators.

After a spirited debate of all the evidence and issues relating to warm-blooded dinosaurs, the Washington meeting ended without a consensus. A summary of the meeting, a work titled *A Cold Look at the Warm-Blooded Dinosaurs*, published in 1980, showed that the experts remained sharply divided. "No . . . resolution of the controversy

over whether dinosaurs were scaled-up, cold-blooded reptiles or warm-blooded . . . 'mammals' is reached here, although the weight of current opinion lies between the extremes." Few scientists have changed their minds since. Ostrom has conceded that many dinosaurs might have displayed warm-blooded behavior because of their large body mass. But he remains convinced that small carnivores such as *Deinonychus* were reptiles that somehow developed true warm-bloodedness. "There is a lot of suspicion out there," he says, "that some or most of these animals were . . . very different from any living reptiles, perhaps more like mammals or birds. Unhappily, we'll never know."

Avian Ancestry: The Case for Flying Dinosaurs

The debate over warm-blooded dinosaurs proved to be only the first of the modern revisionist arguments about these creatures. In the 1970s the warm blood controversy helped to resurrect an old idea that had been first suggested, and then quickly rejected, in the late 1860s. This was the hypothesis that the avians, or birds, developed directly from dinosaurs. Once again, revisionist John Ostrom found himself in the thick of the debate. He and a large number of supporters pointed out that both new evidence and reassessments of older specimens suggested that certain dinosaurs had evolved wings and feathers and learned to fly. This was a revolutionary idea. If true, it meant that in a sense dinosaurs had not become extinct, that birds were their living descendants. And by studying birds, scientists might be able to learn much about dinosaurs that otherwise would be difficult or impossible to discern.

Feathers, Wings, and Wishbones

The original suggestion of a bird-dinosaur link came shortly after an unusual discovery made in 1861 by workers in a limestone quarry in southern Germany. It was the fossilized skeleton of what at first appeared to be a small reptile. But on examining the specimen, German scientist Hermann von Meyer noticed fossilized impressions of feathers and wings in the rock surrounding the bones. This prompted him to name the creature *Archaeopteryx*, meaning "ancient wing." The idea of a flying reptile from the Mesozoic era was not unusual; scientists were already familiar with the *Pterodactyl* and other pterosaurs. What astonished von Meyer were the feathers. Pterosaurs had no feathers, which are exclusive to birds, and scientists previously had not suspected that birds had

The remains of the so-called "London" Archaeopteryx *clearly show the imprints of feathers and wings.*

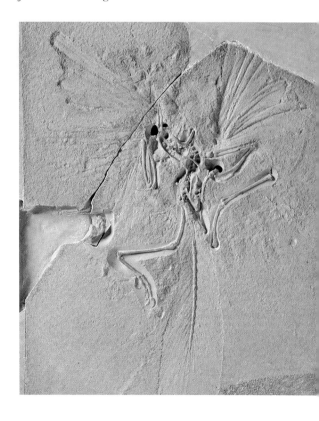

An artist's conception of what Archaeopteryx *looked like in life. It probably used its long, flat tail as a rudder to help stabilize itself during flight.*

developed so early. But von Meyer believed the evidence for the creature being a bird was inescapable. According to biologist Barry Cox:

> The surprising, fortunate feature is that *Archaeopteryx* was fossilized in such fine-grained sediments that the clear impression of its feathers can be seen, spread around the skeleton. Both the individual feathers, and the shape of the wings that they formed, are exactly like those found in living, actively flying birds. So there is little doubt that *Archaeopteryx* was not merely a passive, gliding animal [like the reptilian pterosaurs]. This conclusion is supported by the fact that it possessed a wishbone, which in living birds forms one of the attachment sites for the flight muscles.

There was little doubt, then, that *Archaeopteryx* was a bird, one of the earliest, perhaps even *the* earliest, to develop. But it was the creature's distinct reptilian features that gave scientists pause. A few remarked on how closely this ancient bird's skeleton resembled those of certain dinosaurs. Renowned paleontologist Thomas Henry Huxley said that in particular *Archaeopteryx* looked like the small carnivorous dinosaur *Compsognathus*. Huxley pointed out that *Compsognathus* was bipedal like birds and also had very birdlike ankles and feet. He stated:

> It is impossible to look at the conformation [shape] of this strange reptile and to doubt that it hopped or walked, in an erect or semi-erect position, after the manner of a bird, to which its long neck, slight head, and small anterior [front] limbs must have given it an extraordinary resemblance.

Huxley did not suggest that *Archaeopteryx* had descended from *Compsognathus*. Instead, he believed it likely that the two beasts were close cousins, that they had both evolved from a common dinosaurian ancestor. As further evidence for the bird-dinosaur link,

Huxley cited the birdlike shape of many fossilized Mesozoic dinosaur tracks. "The important truth which these tracks reveal," he said, "is, that at the commencement of the Mesozoic epoch [era], bipedal animals existed which had the feet of birds, and walked in the same erect or semi-erect fashion."

The Debate Killed, Then Revived

Huxley's ideas about avian origins eventually lost support in the scientific community. By the 1890s, so many new and variously shaped dinosaurs had been discovered that the debate over which creature had evolved from which had become confused. Then in the 1920s the respected Danish scientist Gerhard Heilmann rejected the bird-dinosaur link outright in his book, *The Origin of Birds*. Heilmann pointed out that dinosaurs had no wishbones. Nor did they have collarbones that might have developed into wishbones. The lack of these bones, he concluded,

Compsognathus was one of the smallest of all dinosaurs—probably about the size of a hen. It used its long outstretched tail to maintain its balance while running.

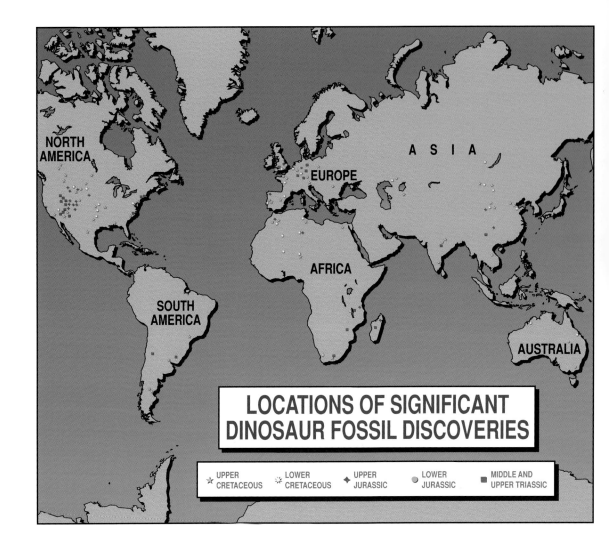

LOCATIONS OF SIGNIFICANT DINOSAUR FOSSIL DISCOVERIES

★ UPPER CRETACEOUS ☆ LOWER CRETACEOUS ◆ UPPER JURASSIC ● LOWER JURASSIC ■ MIDDLE AND UPPER TRIASSIC

"would in itself be sufficient to prove that these saurians could not possibly be ancestors of birds." According to Heilmann, birds had evolved from primitive reptiles that lived before the dinosaurs. The resemblance between birds and dinosaurs, he suggested, was the result of "convergent" evolution, that is, two groups developing by chance along similar lines from similar ancestors. Heilmann had firmly closed the door on a direct relationship between dinosaurs and birds.

However, that door loudly reopened in the early 1970s. In the heat of popular dinosaur revisionism, John Ostrom revived the debate about the bird-dinosaur link. He pointed out that Heilmann's argument about the missing collarbones no longer had weight. Some theropods, a group of predatory bipedal dinosaurs that included *Coelophysis*, *Compsognathus*, and *T. rex*, had been found to possess collarbones. Anyway, Ostrom argued, that was only a minor point. He stated that a detailed ex-

amination of several *Archaeopteryx* specimens had shown that they had more
than twenty features in common with
theropods. Zoologist David Norman explains:

> Some of Ostrom's most telling points in
> favor of a theropod ancestry for *Ar-
> chaeopteryx* and therefore of birds can
> be summarized as follows. First, he
> claimed that the hips of *Archaeopteryx*
> were not bird-like at all but rather were
> crushed into the bird-like arrangement
> during fossilization; in life, therefore,
> they may have closely resembled the ar-
> rangement seen in the theropod di-
> nosaurs. Secondly, the forelimbs of
> theropods and *Archaeopteryx* are remark-
> ably similar down to the minutest detail
> and thirdly, the hindlimbs and feet of
> *Archaeopteryx* are also very similar to
> those of theropods.

These and other similarities, Ostrom argued, constituted strong evidence that the first birds evolved directly from small theropods. In 1975, he
asked:

> Is it more probable that *Archaeopteryx*
> acquired the large number of . . . thero-
> pod characters by convergence or in
> parallel [evolution] at the same time
> that these same features were being ac-
> quired by some . . . theropods—pre-
> sumably from a common ancestor? Or
> is it more likely that these many . . .
> characters are common to some small
> theropods and *Archaeopteryx* because *Ar-
> chaeopteryx* evolved directly from such a
> theropod? There is absolutely no ques-
> tion in my mind that the last explana-
> tion is far more probable.

Ostrom presented his views on avian
ancestry at a 1984 conference in which
experts from around the world met in
Germany to discuss *Archaeopteryx*. Ostrom found that a majority of his colleagues agreed with him that a definite
link existed between dinosaurs and
birds. A few scientists were quite vocal
in their disagreement, however. Larry
Martin, a bird paleontologist at the University of Kansas, for example, stated:

> I don't think birds derived from di-
> nosaurs. The dino argument doesn't
> stand up. You stick a finger into it, it
> goes right through. . . . The people who
> argue that birds are related to di-
> nosaurs use features that aren't gener-
> ally found in all dinosaurs, and most of
> these dinosaurs are very late in the geo-
> logical record.

In other words, the dinosaurs who most
resembled *Archaeopteryx* evolved too late
and so did not have time to develop
into this first bird.

Other opponents of Ostrom's views
claimed that birds could not have descended from theropods because of the
placement of birds' fingers, which are
hidden inside the wings. According to
this view, birds' fingers do not extend
from the wrist in the same order as
theropods' fingers did. If birds came
from dinosaurs, the order should be the
same in both.

Unusual Bone Fragments

Another argument against the bird-
dinosaur link was raised in 1985 after
paleontologist Sankar Chatterjee discovered some unusual bone fragments in
Texas. Chatterjee believed that the
small hollow bones belonged to an ancient bird, which he named *Protoavis*, or
"first bird." The challenge for Ostrom
and his supporters was that Chatterjee's
specimens were about 225 million years
old. This means that *Protoavis* lived at

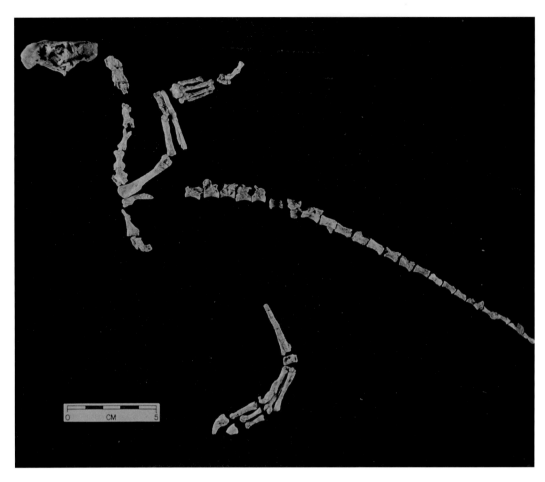

The bones of Protoavis, *believed by paleontologist Sankar Chatterjee to be the world's first bird.*

the dawn of the Mesozoic era, when early dinosaurs were just appearing, and therefore birds had already been evolving for some time. In that case, modern birds would have evolved originally from *Protoavis* and not from *Archaeopteryx*, which developed much later. However, the vast majority of experts did not agree that Chatterjee's bones belonged to a bird. The consensus of opinion was that the creature was a small early dinosaur and that *Archaeopteryx* remained the best candidate for the honor of being the world's first bird.

The Origins of Flight

But while the supporters of the bird-dinosaur link were in the majority, they knew they could never win over their critics without answering a crucial question: How did dinosaurs actually develop flight? An acceptable explanation for how their forelimbs slowly changed into wings had to be found. Northern Arizona University scientist Gerald Caple and some colleagues studied the problem and offered a possible solution, summarized here by John Wilford:

They said that [bipedal dinosaurs], running and lunging after prey, could have used their forelimbs for balance, as humans do when making a broad jump. Such controlling motions resemble a rudimentary flight stroke, which is rather like a lazy figure-eight. If such a stroke were made with . . . feathered forelimbs, air would rush over and under the wing at different rates, thereby creating lift and prolonging the jump.

According to this scenario, the shape of the creatures' feathered forelimbs slowly changed over many generations to heighten the success of this hunting strategy. The jumps became increasingly long and high until the hunters were actually able to remain airborne for extended periods. The eventual result was wings and powered flight.

Although this explanation was acceptable to Ostrom and many other experts, some others believed it did not satisfactorily show how theropods might have developed feathers in the first place. Columbia University biologist Walter J. Bock suggested an alternate view. It explained the development of feathers, as well as why birds ended up dwelling and nesting in trees. Initially, says Bock, small dinosaurs climbed trees to escape predators.

> Because there are fewer predators in the trees than on the ground, proto-birds might have stayed there longer and longer, in [colder, windier] conditions that favored the development of an efficient surface layer of insulation, and, eventually, a complete body covering of feathers.

Dryptosaurus, also called Laelaps, *"the leaper," because of its ability to jump high off the ground. Small dinosaurs with similar ability may eventually have taken to the air.*

This painting by Neave Parker of a Hypsilophodon *in a tree was based on an incorrect description of the creature's foot, suggesting that its claws were designed for grasping branches.*

According to Bock, these creatures learned to jump from tree to tree and from trees to ground. In time, their feathered forelimbs provided them with lift and they developed flight. Because their home was in the trees, they nested there instead of on the ground as their ancestors had.

If Bock's view is correct, it does not necessarily follow that the one put forward by Caple's team is wrong. In fact, a number of scientists believe that both the ground-runner and tree-dweller versions of the origins of flight are probable. That means that different groups of small dinosaurs may have taken different paths to reach the same goal—life in the air. Which path *Archaeopteryx* may have taken is unknown.

Although the question of the bird-dinosaur link remains officially open, this theory of avian ancestry has become the most accepted in the scientific community. It is supported by a great deal of fossil and anatomic evidence. If true, Ostrom points out, it means that the dinosaurs "did not become extinct without descendants." That leads to a somewhat disturbing but thoroughly intriguing possibility: The feathered friends perched on the backyard birdbath might be, in reality, living dinosaurs.

Good Mother: Social Life in a Mud Nest

The revisionist debates about warm-blooded and bird-related dinosaurs focused scientists' attention increasingly on the physical behavior of these creatures. Researchers theorized about the dinosaurs' activity levels, how they ran and jumped, what and how often they ate, and so on. Soon, studies and discussions of physical behavior expanded to include new ideas about social behavior. This was new and unknown territory for scientists, for up until the 1970s they had never considered the possibility that dinosaurs might have been social animals. The traditional and accepted view was that, because they were big reptiles, dinosaurs were cold, slow, lazy, and stupid. In this scenario, dinosaurs, like most other reptiles, neither cared for their young nor herded or hunted together as mammals do. In short, dinosaurs were mostly solitary, antisocial beasts.

However, stimulated by revisionist debate and some unexpected and remarkable field discoveries in the 1970s and 1980s, a markedly new view of dinosaur behavior emerged. Research showed that many of these creatures had complex and varied social lives much like those of some modern animals. Evidence showed conclusively that at least some dinosaurs cared for their young, roamed in herds, and hunted in packs. They may even have communicated by making sounds. All of these behaviors are normally associated with active, intelligent, and social creatures.

In this painting titled "Defending the Nest," a Protoceratops *tries to ward off a hungry* Velociraptor.

The Two Medicine Babies

The discovery of social dinosaurs began in earnest in the summer of 1978 in northern Montana. Two young fossil hunters, John Horner and Bob Makela, had been exploring for several weeks with little success. Neither had college degrees in paleontology or were recognized scientists. When he was not out snooping for bones, Horner helped scientists clean and prepare prehistoric specimens at Princeton University's Museum of Natural History in New Jersey. Makela made his living teaching high school in a small Montana town. No one expected these amateurs to make one of the greatest scientific finds of the century.

But Horner and Makela did just that. One day in midsummer the pair examined some small fossil bones that the owners of a local shop had found on a nearby ranch. Horner may have been an amateur, but he had learned a great deal about dinosaurs both in the field and while working at the museum, and he also had an unusually sharp eye. "You're not going to believe this," he told Makela excitedly, "but I think these are pieces of a baby duck-billed dinosaur." This in itself was a significant discovery because very few remains of juvenile or baby dinosaurs had previously been found.

The two men hurried to the ranch where the fossils had been collected. Located near the Teton River and the town of Great Falls, the area of Montana grasslands and mudstone is known to geologists as the "Two Medicine Formation." Mudstone is a rocky substance that forms when layers of ancient mud

Fossil hunter John Horner displays some of the Maiasaurus *eggs he discovered in Montana.*

harden over time. Because dead animals lying in the fresh mud might be covered over and undergo fossilization, mudstone is a good place to look for fossils. Horner and Makela began digging in the Two Medicine Formation mudstone and in only a few days made an exciting discovery: a hardened mud nest containing fifteen fossilized baby dinosaurs. The specimens, the first young dinosaurs ever found in a nest, were about three feet long. The nest itself was about six feet in diameter and three feet deep.

Perhaps the most unusual thing about the fossil babies was that they were not recent hatchlings. The prevailing view at the time was that dinosaurs, being reptiles, largely abandoned their young after birth. So the young immediately left the nest and went out to face survival on their own. Following this scenario, Horner's and Makela's babies must have died and become fossilized in the nest right after birth. But as Horner later wrote:

> The dinosaurs from the nest were not so young . . . that they had hatched out of the egg and keeled over dead. The tendons that run along the spine and keep the tail off the ground were already hard, or ossified, not flexible as they would be at the time of hatching. And, an even stronger sign . . . was that the teeth were worn—some of them almost three-quarters gone. . . . Clearly, the young had been eating for some time.

If the hatchlings had remained in the nest for weeks or months and were eating and growing, where did they obtain food? Horner realized that there could be only one answer: their mother had nurtured and fed them!

No Mere Lizard

The discoveries Horner and Makela made later that summer and in the next

This reconstruction of a Maiasaurus *nest shows both intact eggs and recent hatchlings.*

The relative difference in size between Maiasaurus *adults and babies is illustrated by this photo of their skulls.*

few years confirmed that these dinosaurs had indeed cared for their infant offspring. The men found the remains of an entire colony of nesting dinosaurs in the Two Medicine Formation mudstone. Digging at a mound they dubbed "Egg Mountain," they unearthed ten nests, each bearing as many as twenty-four eggs. In all, they found more than three hundred dinosaur eggs in nests and more than sixty skeletons of babies, juveniles, and their parents, all of the same species. Horner named this new dinosaur, a member of the herbivorous duck-billed family, *Maiasaurus*, meaning "good mother lizard."

But the *Maiasaurus* was no mere lizard. In his book *Digging Dinosaurs*, Horner described various aspects of the creature's social order he deduced from the evidence found in the nests:

> The sites of those 6-foot-wide nests were equally spaced, 23 feet apart. Twenty-three feet is the average length of adult *maiasaurs*. . . . Among ground-nesting birds now [such as penguins], it's common for nests to be separated by the length of an adult bird's outstretched wings. This seems to allow for the maximum of togetherness and the minimum

of interference. If the maiasaurs were behaving like birds, as it seems they were, this means that they not only picked the same place to lay eggs but also had a social system of sorts, with what you might call prescribed "personal space."

Horner believes that *Maiasaurus* and other duck-billed dinosaurs established nesting colonies partly for mutual protection. With many adults congregating in the same area, it would have been more difficult for predators to get at the babies. Horner and Makela found clear evidence of such predators. "The maiasaurs were not alone in their world, or in their nesting ground," says Horner:

There were also small, wolf-size predatory dinosaurs, whose fossils we have found. . . . I suspect they raided the nests in groups, trying to avoid the adult maiasaurs and snatch a baby or two. The inevitable presence of these predators is another reason to believe the young stayed in the nest. Baby alligators get eaten in great numbers, and the young maiasaurs were nowhere near as toothy as they are. A bunch of baby maiasaurs walking around alone would have been like meals-on-wheels for the carnivores.

Clearly then, good mother dinosaurs not only nurtured their young, but also exhibited group mutual protection be-

The *"good mother" lizard oversees its hatchlings in this depiction of a typical* Maiasaurus *nest. Despite the parent's watchful eye, some of the babies will inevitably fall prey to roving predators.*

haviors normally associated mainly with warm-blooded, social creatures.

In fact, Horner found other evidence that strongly supported the argument that some dinosaurs were warm-blooded. He analyzed the bone development of the babies he had found and concluded that the young hatchlings had undergone rapid growth. This suggested the fast metabolism of a warm-blooded animal, as opposed to the sluggish metabolism and slow growth of typical cold-blooded reptiles. This surprised Horner, who before had not been a strong supporter of the warm-blooded view. "I used to argue with [Bob] Bakker [chief proponent of dinosaur warm-bloodedness] all the time," Horner admitted. "And I still argue with him on some points, but it's hard to explain what I'm seeing [in the babies' bone growth] any other way." This conclusion, Horner and other scientists contend, is certainly consistent with the nesting evidence. If the maiasaurs were indeed warm-blooded, then it is not so surprising that they engaged in various kinds of social behavior.

This model of a baby Maiasaurus *hatching from its egg case was based on the most recent evidence from the Montana nests.*

A depiction of an embryonic Hypsilophodon *curled tightly within its unbroken egg case.*

In addition to nurturing young, other such behaviors apparently included herding and migrating. Many modern warm-blooded herbivores, such as buffalo and antelope, band together in herds for mutual protection. In 1984, Horner and some colleagues made an intriguing discovery proving that maiasaurs did the same. At a Two Medicine Formation site called Willow Creek, they found an unprecedented mass grave. As Horner later recalled:

> There was no question. . . . We had one huge bed of maiasaur bones—and nothing but maiasaur bones—stretching a mile and a quarter east to west and a quarter-mile north to south. Judging from the concentration of bones in various pits, there were up to 30 million fossil fragments in that area. At a conservative estimate, we had discovered the tomb of 10,000 dinosaurs. . . . What could such a deposit represent?

There were no nests and very few baby maiasaurs in the deposit. The only explanation for so many mature individuals of the same dinosaur species coming together this way, Horner reasoned, was that they were members of a large herd. Eventually, Horner and other experts concluded that hot poisonous gases from a nearby volcanic eruption killed the herd. After sun, wind, and mud from floodwaters took their toll on the corpses, a layer of volcanic ash covered the remains and they slowly fossilized.

The discovery of more large bone beds and other evidence subsequently confirmed that at least some dinosaurs, certainly many herbivores, herded and migrated from place to place in search of food. Modern herbivore herds attract predators such as lions and wild dogs, of course. And the same was undoubtedly true of dinosaur herds, which fell prey to vicious meat-eaters such as *Deinonychus* and *T. rex.* For a long time,

the antisocial view of dinosaurs held that such carnivores traveled and hunted alone. But recent evidence shows this was not always the case. Ralph Molnar, curator of the Queensland Museum in Brisbane, Australia, points out in his essay "The Behavior of Predatory Dinosaurs":

> Although some theropods probably hunted individually, there is evidence for hunting in packs as well. Fossils of several theropods . . . such as *Coelophysis, Dilophosaurus* and *Syntarsus,* have been found in groups, of from 3 to several hundred individuals. And there are tracks that indicate several individuals traveled and hunted together at the same time.

In this painting, a pack of bipedal hunters causes a herd of large plant eaters to panic and stampede.

DINOSAUR HORNS AND CLUBS

A Triceratops *may have used its prominent horns for attracting mates more often than for defense.*

The realization that dinosaurs behaved in many ways like modern animals has prompted scientists to rethink numerous old assumptions about dinosaurs. For instance, some researchers have challenged traditional notions about horned dinosaurs like *Triceratops* and dinosaurs with bony clubs on their tails like *Ankylosaurus*. The common wisdom had always been that these appendages had evolved primarily for use as weapons. Revisionist John Horner, for one, disagrees. In his book *Digging Dinosaurs*, he writes:

> I believe sexual attraction, not defense, was the reason these characteristics evolved. . . . To me there is no subject on which so much nonsense has been heard as defense among dinosaurs. It's not just the paintings of *Triceratops* battling *Tyrannosaurus* made for popular consumption. Scientists, too, assume that horns and clubs were weapons. This is seldom the case among animals today, and I doubt things were different in the Cretaceous. All the existing herbivores with great antlers developed them to attract mates and conduct sexual combat between males. Occasionally, very occasionally, the horns may be used . . . to fend off a predator, but I doubt that this usually succeeds. An elk is better off using its feet rather than its horns to attack wolves. Bighorn sheep use their magnificent horns to butt each other. Elk and moose do the same. And so, I bet, did *Triceratops*.

Before these discoveries, scientists had associated pack hunting, which shows a high order of social organization and intelligence, mainly with mammals such as lions, hyenas, and dogs. Here was proof that carnivorous as well as herbivorous dinosaurs were social creatures that used certain behaviors to benefit their individual groups. For instance, one *Deinonychus*, the size of a small man, may have had trouble bringing down a two-to-three-ton adult duckbill, which could have defended itself with swipes of its massive tail. But consider a coordinated attack by four or more *Deinonychuses*. The larger animal would have no chance at all against the pack, its members slashing out with their razorlike claws as they leapt at their prey from all sides.

Scientists have also considered another aspect of dinosaur socialization—how some species may have communicated in a primitive fashion using sounds. Modern herding animals employ various bleats and bellows to warn

In this painting, adult maiasaurs wander through a haze of volcanic dust that settles over their nesting site.

others of approaching predators and a number of creatures use sounds to attract members of the opposite sex. John Horner has suggested that *Maiasaurus*, among other dinosaurs, made similar noises by blowing air through the chambers inside its nose. According to John Wilford, "This could have produced a deep tuba sound." To fend off attack, Wilford says, herding dinosaurs may have relied on "croaking or barking or sounding their tubas to alert others of imminent peril." Canadian paleontologist Philip Currie speculates that dinosaur noises sounded something like a French horn. He explains that some duck-billed species had hollow chambers inside the crests at the tops of their heads, spaces through which they might have pushed bursts of air, resulting in loud, mellow tones.

A Day in the Cretaceous

The likelihood that at least some dinosaurs used sounds to communicate is one more reason to abandon old notions of their being primitive, dull-witted beasts. In fact, only highly advanced, intelligent animals could have engaged in social behaviors such as caring for young, herding and sounding warnings for mutual protection, and pack-hunting. Thus, modern science sees dinosaurs in a new light. As is true of animals today, they were highly diversified creatures who interacted with each other in various and complex ways. And new reconstructions of the dinosaurs' daily lives reflect this revisionist view. In his book *Kings of Creation*, Don Lessem paints the following picture of a typical afternoon in the late Cretaceous period:

From a forested upland where the duck-bill dinosaurs spent spring and summer hatching and tending their fast-growing babies, a vast herd proceeds by long, two-legged strides, south along the highlands. Heads bob as they slowly march. Elaborately ornamented males stride in front, issuing rumbling toots from their nasal tubes to keep stragglers in line. Other adults guard

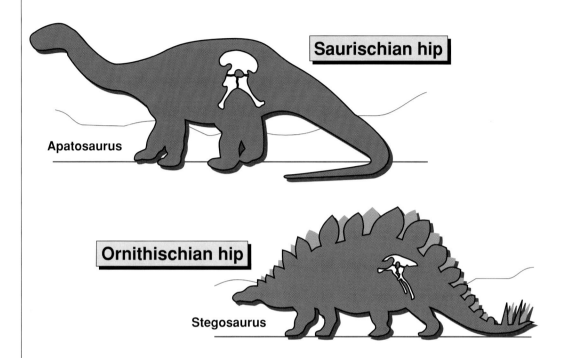

DINOSAUR HIP STRUCTURE

Saurischian hip

Apatosaurus

Ornithischian hip

Stegosaurus

Scientists classify dinosaurs in two basic groups according to hip structure. The first group, the saurischians, or "lizard-hipped" dinosaurs, had hip bones arranged like those of reptiles. The second group, the ornithiscians, or "bird-hipped" dinosaurs, had hip bones similar to those of birds.

the flanks of the herd and the half-size juveniles at its center. All are alert to the sight and smell of packs of small hunters and the huge and dreaded tyrannosaurs. Browsing as they head to the subtropical shore, the duck-bills pass other residents of this productive land . . . clusters of squat, young armored dinosaurs [and] . . . large herds of horned dinosaurs, whose huge, bony [neck] frills point upward as they noisily munch, faces in the brush.

The highly diverse and social creatures roaming this ancient landscape had no way of knowing that their kind was doomed. Eventually, the Cretaceous calm would be shattered and dinosaurs everywhere would disappear forever. Millions of years later, the search for the mysterious cause of their demise would lead human researchers to the most exciting bit of dinosaur revisionism yet.

Cosmic Intruder: The K-T Event and the Dinosaurs' Demise

Many puzzles about dinosaurs and their way of life remain. Yet perhaps the most baffling and compelling question about dinosaurs, for scientists and the public alike, is not how these creatures lived, but rather, how they died. Their mass extinction was both untimely and strange. It was untimely because during the late Cretaceous period dinosaurs, after a reign of more than 150 million years, still easily dominated the natural world. All over the earth other creatures, including the still tiny mammals, were no match for them. Dinosaurs seemed to be the main characters in nature's greatest success story and were highly unlikely candidates for extinction.

The dinosaurs' death was strange because it was unusually sudden and wide ranging. The extinction of species is a normal occurrence in nature. In fact, far more species have become extinct in past ages than exist on earth today. But as a rule various species belonging to a related group die off gradually, leaving the group as a whole intact. Bird species such as the giant moa, the dodo, and the passenger pigeon became extinct, for example, but most birds are still around. By contrast, all of the dinosaurs—every species in every corner of the world—died abruptly and at about the same time. In geologic terms, this mass dying ended the Cretaceous period, which was followed by the Tertiary period, in which mammals inherited the earth. So scientists refer to the division between the two periods as the Cretaceous-Tertiary, or K-T, boundary. (The letter *K* is used to avoid confusion with the earlier Cambrian and Carboniferous periods.) No

In this reconstructed scene from the late Cretaceous period, a T-rex (foreground) bellows at a group of potential prey, including two multi-horned styracosaurs.

A hypothetical scene showing non-dinosaurian inhabitants of Cretaceous times. A long-necked Elasmosaurus *confronts another large marine reptile,* Tylosaurus, *while a bat-winged* Pteranodon *glides overhead.*

dinosaur fossils have ever been found in strata above the K-T boundary, leading scientists to the inescapable conclusion that these creatures died suddenly and completely.

Arguments and Counterarguments

Until the 1970s, the cause of this great dying was one of modern science's major unexplained mysteries. Scientists offered many different explanations for the dinosaurs' demise, but most of these had little or no evidence to support them. And for each new argument there seemed to be valid and logical counterarguments. Typical was the once popular notion that dinosaurs perished because rodentlike mammals raided their nests and ate all the eggs. As David Norman aptly points out:

> A few moments' reflection are probably all that is needed to come to a decision about this particular theory. In the first place, it is exceedingly improbable that the change to an egg-eating diet by mammals should have caused the ex-

tinction of *all* dinosaur species; after all we cannot even be sure they all laid eggs! Secondly, many egg-eating species are known today but these show no sign whatever of causing the extinction of their prey; indeed it is biological 'common sense' not to cause the extinction of the organisms that you feed upon. Otherwise you will surely hasten your own end.

Another weakness of the egg-eating idea was that it did not explain the huge scope of the K-T extinctions. The dinosaurs were not the only group that suffered in this biological catastrophe, often referred to as the K-T "event." More than 38 percent of all species of marine animals, including the big swimming reptiles such as the plesiosaurs, also died out entirely. And on land, at least a third of the mammals and large numbers of the amphibian, reptilian, and plant species met their end. Clearly, mammalian consumption of dinosaur eggs cannot account for the extinction of sea animals, plants, and other mammals.

Other theories had similar weaknesses. For instance, some scientists

CONTINENTAL DRIFTING

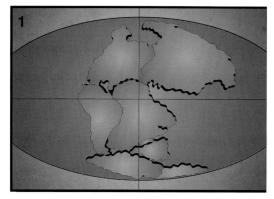 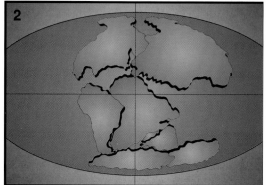

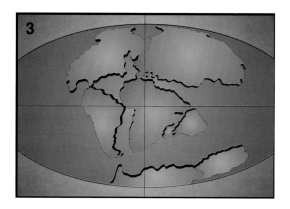

Over the course of many millions of years, the earth's continents have slowly moved and changed shape. This "continental drifting" affected the migration patterns of dinosaurs. In the Triassic period, most of the earth's land masses were connected to each other (1), allowing dinosaurs to roam freely throughout the world. In the Jurassic period, the continents began to split up (2), but land bridges still allowed open migrations. In the Cretaceous period, however, most large land masses became separated as they are today (3), confining certain dinosaur groups to specific geographical regions.

suggested that dinosaurs' brains remained tiny while their bodies grew huge. According to this view, the beasts were too stupid to adapt to normal environmental changes and so they died out. This idea, like the egg-eating one, did not explain the plant extinctions. Also, a number of dinosaurs had small bodies with relatively large brains, among them crafty pack-hunters like *Deinonychus*, and were most likely highly adaptable to change.

One of the most popular theories blamed the extinctions on climatic change. Supposedly, worldwide tropical climates grew colder and the dinosaurs, being cold-blooded, could not adapt. The counterargument is that climatic changes were gradual and dinosaurs should have had time to migrate to the remaining warm regions. Besides, crocodiles, turtles, and many other cold-blooded creatures survived the changes. Why not the dinosaurs? Among the numerous other theories advanced were poor diet, poison plants, plagues, parasites, toxic volcanic gases, excess oxygen buildup by plants, floods, mountain-building, and changes in the earth's rotation. But none of these clearly and convincingly explained the immensity, diversity, and suddenness of the K-T extinctions.

A Clue in the Clays

In the mid-1970s, Nobel Prize-winning scientist Harold C. Urey proposed still another tentative theory for the extinctions. He suggested that an extraterrestrial body such as a comet or large meteorite might have struck the earth with the force of thousands of nuclear bombs. This, he said, might have killed the dinosaurs by suddenly and sharply raising global temperatures. At first, because no physical proof for such an impact yet existed, few scientists were willing to accept the idea of a cosmic intruder bringing about the great dying. Without some kind of clear, compelling evidence, they said, it was just another interesting bit of speculation.

As it happened, the first piece of compelling evidence for a cosmic collision was not long in coming. In 1979, another Nobel winner, physicist Dr. Luis Alvarez, and his son, geologist Walter Alvarez, described their discovery of high concentrations of the element iridium in K-T boundary clays and rocks in Italy, Denmark, and New Zealand. Iridium is a dark, heavy metal. Paleontologist

A T-rex *is interrupted from devouring its duck-billed prey by the brilliant flash of the descending cosmic intruder. The big carnivore will never finish its last meal.*

David M. Raup explains in his book *Extinction: Bad Genes or Bad Luck*:

> Whereas iridium is common in some meteorites, it is vanishingly rare in the earth's crust. The Alvarez group quite logically concluded that the K-T deposit [of iridium] was formed of debris from the impact of an asteroid or rocky comet. So much iridium was present that the impacting object . . . must have had a diameter of ten kilometers [six miles]. Because of the coincidence in timing with a big mass extinction, they proposed that the environmental effects of the impact caused the extinction.

The only other way to explain the rich iridium layer was the simultaneous eruption of dozens or even hundreds of volcanoes worldwide, a highly improbable event. Thus, the Alvarezes' find was strong evidence indeed for a cosmic impact. This explanation for the K-T event began to attract an increasing number of scientists from a number of different fields.

Nuclear Winter

Some of these researchers calculated the intruder's possible size, speed, energy of impact, and other factors and constructed likely scenarios for the catastrophe. In the most popular version, a rocky object six miles in diameter hurtled out of the sky, traveling at the incredible speed of fifteen miles per second. The cosmic missile sped through the earth's lower atmosphere in less than a second. Its chances of striking the ocean were about 70 percent, because that is the proportion of the earth's surface covered by water. On striking either land or the sea bottom with stupendous

force, the object gouged out a hole as much as ten times its size—a crater perhaps sixty or more miles wide. "For either kind of impact," states science writer Dr. Donald Goldsmith,

> most of the material ejected by the impact would be dust and grit, heated by the impact to hundreds of thousands of degrees, which would rise through the atmosphere. . . . Much of the hot dust . . . would diffuse around the stratosphere [upper atmosphere] in less than an hour. Within a few hours after the collision, the earth would be surrounded by a heavy veil of atmospheric dust, and a long night would fall around our planet.

In this "nuclear winter," the term scientists often use to describe such a scenario, the pall of dust blocked incoming sunlight for months. The temperatures plummeted to levels well below zero, even in the tropics. With light levels reduced to as little as 1 percent of normal, photosynthesis, the chemical process vital to plant growth, ceased, and much of the world's vegetation shriveled. Unable to find enough food, active herbivorous dinosaurs quickly perished. Their death doomed the carnivores who normally preyed on them, and soon the landscape was littered with the corpses of millions of dinosaurs and other creatures. Some mammals, able to burrow underground or hibernate to escape the cold, managed to survive until the sun returned. Crocodiles, turtles, and other reptiles that could live submerged in mud or river bottoms also survived.

The devastating nuclear winter was likely just one of the catastrophic effects of the giant impact. A sea strike would surely have produced huge tsunamis, or tidal waves. These struck coasts around

Several specimens of Struthiomimus, *a small bipedal Cretaceous dinosaur, run panic stricken through a forest fire ignited by the K-T impact.*

the world and rushed inland for miles, annihilating every living thing in their paths. Some researchers believe that the planetary cloud layer produced lethal concentrations of acid rain, which burned the dinosaurs' hairless hides. Others say the impact ignited huge global forest fires that swept across the continents. Still other impact theory supporters, says *Science* magazine's Virginia Morell, "argue that the period of dark cold may have been 5 to 10 years, rather than just a few months—and even the most highly winterized dinosaur would have had trouble coping with that."

The "Smoking Gun"

The main reason that so many scientists have embraced the collision theory is that it seems to explain nearly all aspects of the K-T event, something no other theory has done. It accounts for the iridium layers found in K-T boundary strata in many parts of the world. It also explains why so many land species, both plant and animal, died out and shows logically how some species survived. The theory even accounts for the destruction of large marine reptiles like *Mosasaurus* and *Ichthyosaurus*. A sudden

decrease in water temperature was accompanied by a temporary but serious disruption of the ocean food chain. The shutoff of sunlight killed masses of plankton, tiny creatures that swarm near the surface of the oceans. Because small fish ate the plankton and the big marine reptiles ate the fish, the reptiles' food supply was cut off.

Although the impact idea was very persuasive, a small minority of scientists remained skeptical about it during the 1980s. Perhaps their main criticism was that no impact crater of the right age and size had yet been found. Of the roughly 120 known impact craters on earth, they pointed out, none matched the conditions of the proposed K-T impact. Until this "smoking gun" of the K-T catastrophe could be located, the collision theory puzzle would remain incomplete.

In 1989 the puzzle's pieces quickly began to come together. Scientists Alan Hildebrand and William Boynton of the University of Arizona found evidence that huge tsunamis had swept the coasts of Mexico, Cuba, and the southern United States at about the time of the K-T event. This seemed to suggest that a large object had plunged into the Caribbean Sea. Chemical analyses of

Dale Russell's and Ron Séguin's intelligent dinosauroid and its ancestor, Stenonychosaurus.

In 1982, Canadian scientist Dale A. Russell attempted to answer the intriguing question, what if the K-T impact had not occurred and the dinosaurs had lived? Because they were already the undisputed masters of the earth, he reasoned, they likely would have remained the planet's dominant life-form as they continued to evolve. Thus, large mammals, including human beings, would not have developed. Russell proposed that some dinosaurs might eventually have evolved intelligence comparable to that of humans. He pointed out that some small late-Cretaceous carnivores, among them the three-foot-tall *Stenonychosaurus*, had unusually large brains for reptiles and were undoubtedly clever hunters. The *Stenonychosaurus* also had an opposable thumb, like apes and humans do. This gave it the potential of developing the ability to use tools, and thereby of one day constructing a civilization. Russell, with the assistance of taxidermist Ron Séguin, constructed a life-size model of the creature's possible intelligent descendant. Russell called it a "dinosauroid."

The men based the creature's physical characteristics on logical scientific assumptions. For instance, because the evolving dinosaur's long, skinny neck could no longer support its steadily enlarging brain and skull, the neck shortened and the head moved over the shoulders for extra support. This gave the dinosauroid bipedal posture like that of humans. And because the tail was no longer necessary to counterbalance the neck, the tail slowly disappeared. The dinosauroid model is on display at the National Museum of Natural Sciences in Ottawa, Canada. It remains a thought-provoking reminder that the course of evolution is subject to random events. Had it not been for a chance meeting between the earth and a wandering chunk of rock long ago, modern civilization might have been built by three-fingered hands.

Caribbean rocks in 1990 also indicated a large Caribbean impact, probably near Mexico's Yucatan peninsula. The search for the dinosaurs' "death star" seemed to be narrowing. Finally, in 1991 researchers from NASA's Ames Research Center and other scientists confirmed the existence of a submerged Yucatan crater. Says Don Lessem:

> The most celebrated scientific detective quest of the decade has now produced a "smoking gun." The presumed dinosaur-killer is a crater 120 miles wide formed by an object from space six miles across slamming into the earth with an impact 10,000 times more powerful than the explosion that would be produced by setting off all the world's atomic weapons simultaneously. The crater has been dubbed Chicxulub. . . . In ancient Mayan [the people who once inhabited the Yucatan], Chicxulub means "tail of the devil."

The Race Is Not to the Swift

Chicxulub's discovery and subsequent studies of the sunken crater have won over most of the collision theory's doubters. However, a few paleontologists remain stubborn holdouts. Robert Bakker, for example, insists that the extinctions happened more gradually, perhaps over the course of a few hundred thousand years. The K-T impact probably reduced the dinosaur population, he admits. But something else, perhaps disease parasites spread by migrating dinosaurs, finally did the creatures in.

But the evidence that the dinosaurs' world ended with a bang, continues to pour in. It now seems highly probable

Two specimens of Corythosaurus, *a 33-foot-long, crested herbivore, are startled by the expanding fireball of the massive K-T impact.*

that these magnificent and terrifying beasts met their doom from an intruder from space. Ironically, it was not their own mistakes or shortcomings that struck them down at the height of their natural power and glory, but an act of blind chance. For scientist Kenneth J. Hsu, this is a potent reminder that attributes such as superior strength and speed do not always ensure success. Even the most powerful are at the mercy of nature's occasional unexpected events and of the ravages of time. "The essence of my perception," he says, "can best be expressed by a quote from the Bible: 'I returned and saw under the sun that the race is not to the swift, nor the battle to the strong . . . but time and chance happen to them all.'"

CHAPTER 8

Future Hunting: Dinosaurs at the Poles and Beyond

After nearly two centuries of dinosaur discovery, the excavation and study of these unusual beasts remains an ongoing process. Whether the next great age of discovery will be as fruitful as previous ones is an open question. The future of dinosaur hunting seems both unlimited and limited, depending on one's point of view. On the one hand, the pace of finding and naming new dinosaur species has increased markedly in recent years. A new species is described and named about every seven weeks. And scientists have identified almost half of all known dinosaur species since the early 1970s. In addition, new computer-based and other advanced technology is making the location and examination of these creatures easier and more accurate.

On the other hand, progress in paleontology is limited by a constant lack of funding. Scientists could make even greater strides if they could launch more expeditions, expand work at current digs, and hire more people to clean, catalog, and study specimens. But research money from governmental and private sources has to be fairly divided among many branches of science, and only so much can be allocated for fossil studies. So dinosaur research remains a relatively modest endeavor. According to John Horner:

> The total amount of money given out by the National Science Foundation to all the . . . paleontologists in the country for research on dinosaurs is no more than $500,000 a year. I can count on my fingers the full-fledged excavations for dinosaur fossils on the North American continent, and half of those are in Alberta, where the [Canadian] government seems to have a soft spot for paleontology.

Fast, Agile, and Clever

Nevertheless, today's dinosaur hunters regularly make up for their limited resources through stubborn determination, clever detective work, and sheer backbreaking labor. Their tireless efforts keep the stream of new dinosaur knowledge flowing to a public still fascinated by dinosaurs. Some of this new

An egg belonging to Troödon, *which had the most birdlike skull structure of any known dinosaur.*

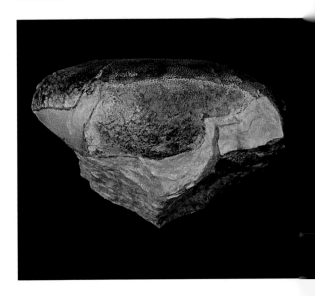

A pair of Troödons, *carrying a captured orodromeos lizard, trot back to their lair where they will devour their meal.*

knowledge comes from reexamining old evidence and seeing it in a new light. For example, the small carnivore *Troödon*, or "wounding tooth," was discovered and cataloged in the 1800s. Only recently, however, have scientists begun to realize how unusual this creature was. Since the revival of the bird-dinosaur link in the 1970s, the search has been on for dinosaurs who exhibited birdlike characteristics. And *Troödon*, researchers recently established, had the most birdlike skull structure of any known dinosaur. Paleontologists continue to search for more *Troödon* remains in hopes of learning more about how dinosaurs evolved into birds.

New studies of *Troödon* may also yield valuable information about dinosaur intelligence. Scientists have known for some time that small pack-hunters like *Deinonychus* were smarter than most other dinosaurs. And *Stenonychosaurus*, with its opposable thumb, was apparently unusually clever. The active, nimble *Troödon* promises to shed new light on the evident superior intellect of some small dinosaur predators. Don Lessem explains:

Statistical measurements have correlated brain size with intelligence in living mammals. To judge from its brain size and by estimated brain-to-body-weight ratio, *Troödon* was at least as smart as an ostrich. And by these standards, *Troödon* appears to have been bright enough to coordinate not only its own keen stereoscopic vision and gripping hands, but to hunt cooperatively as many advanced predators do today. Little troödontids, not huge tyrannosaurs, may have been the most efficient hunters of dinosaur times—fast, agile, and above all, clever.

New Techniques Yield New Finds

Other new dinosaur knowledge is made possible by advancing technology. For instance, some recently developed high-tech field methods make it much easier and less time consuming to locate dinosaur fossils. A kind of radar device that geologists designed to search for specific underground rock formations is now being used to find dinosaurs. The device works by giving off small bursts of radio waves. These bounce off rocks and other underground objects and return to a receiver. Because bone fossils reflect the waves differently than rocks do, the device's operator can tell if ancient bones lie beneath the surface.

Such technology has been very helpful in the search for new fossils and previously unknown species. One of the most exciting ongoing discoveries is that of *Seismosaurus*, or "earth-shaking lizard," named in 1991 by American pa-

Although T-rex, pictured here on the prowl through a Cretaceous forest, was a powerful and frightening hunter, it was probably far less clever and efficient than the smaller, more agile Troödon.

These allosaurs stalk a huge Seismosaurus *through a late Jurassic swamp.*

leontologist David Gillette. *Seismosaurus,* a member of the sauropod family, which includes long-necked giants like *Apatosaurus,* was perhaps the longest dinosaur that ever walked the earth. In answer to the question of just how long it was, Gillette responds:

> The standard answer is, in excess of one hundred and ten feet. . . . We don't have enough information to say absolutely the length; it could be from seventy-five to eighty-five feet up to one hundred seventy feet. I think one hundred forty feet to one hundred fifty is a fair estimate.

Gillette's excavation of *Seismosaurus,* begun at a site in New Mexico in the late 1980s, is expected to continue for some time. This is partly because the bones are so huge and require a great deal of time and effort to remove from the ground and to clean and preserve. Such a challenging project is also expensive. Gillette estimates that it will require at least a million dollars to excavate the creature completely. Simply cleaning the bones unearthed until the end of 1991 is keeping one technician busy for five years at $25,000 a year. Unfortunately, Gillette suffers from the same chronic lack of funding that other fossil hunters do, and the pace of the work remains slower than he would like. "*Seismosaurus* is a project that will last me the rest of my life," he says. And he adds good-naturedly, "I just hope to God I never find another giant sauropod."

A fossilized dinosaur footprint found at Dinosaur Cove in southeastern Australia. The fact that many dinosaur species lived in the area's once cold and dark climate is strong evidence that some dinosaurs were warm-blooded.

In the Cold and the Dark

New discoveries are disclosing not only new sizes and shapes for dinosaurs, but also previously unknown habitats and behaviors that challenge traditional assumptions about these beasts. Some of the most unusual finds in this regard are dinosaur remains near the earth's poles. In the 1980s, scientists began unearthing various dinosaur species at a site called Dinosaur Cove in southeastern Australia. In the Cretaceous period, Australia was joined with Antarctica, the frozen continent that straddles the South Pole. So at the time, the area containing these fossils had a very cool climate. It was not as harsh as Antarctica is today, but the temperature likely remained a little above or below zero for

extended periods, and it snowed often. Even more significantly, the sun remained below the horizon for most of the winter each year. This means that these dinosaurs somehow adapted to prolonged periods of cold and dark, an image that contrasts sharply with the traditional view of lazy dinosaurs sunning themselves on a tropical afternoon. The 1980s also produced similar fossil evidence from above the Arctic Circle in Alaska. Apparently, these northern dinosaurs did not live year-round in the polar region, but rather, regularly migrated to and from the area.

The continuing discovery and examination of new polar dinosaurs raises some important questions: First, how were these creatures able to adapt to such extreme conditions? Some researchers say that this is the best proof yet that at least some dinosaurs were warm-blooded. Most of the Australian polar species found thus far were unusually small; the argument that they were cold-blooded creatures that retained heat through large body mass does not apply here. Even the area's chief predator, a version of the carnivorous *Allosaurus*, was no larger than a human. Until more evidence proves otherwise, warm-bloodedness remains the best way to explain this unusual feat of cold adaptation.

Another question raised by the polar dinosaurs is whether these animals, specially adapted to the cold and dark, might have somehow survived the effects of the K-T cosmic impact. Patricia and Thomas Rich, the chief scientists at the Dinosaur Cove site in Australia, say that this depends on how long the devastating nuclear winter lasted. "One must question," they wrote in 1993,

> whether animals so superbly adapted to the cold and the dark could have been driven to extinction by an artificial winter, such as is supposed to have followed

In this reconstructed view of a Cretaceous landscape, a group of maiasaurs scatters to avoid a hungry Albertosaurus. *A number of dinosaurs managed to survive in the kind of eerie darkness pictured here, suggesting they were highly adaptable creatures.*

a cataclysmic [catastrophic] event at the boundary between the Cretaceous and the Tertiary. . . . We suspect, however, that no such artificial winter could have killed the [polar] dinosaurs unless it lasted for a long time, certainly more than a few months. Otherwise at least a few of the polar dinosaurs would have survived the cataclysm.

Might some of these creatures have survived the K-T event? It is certainly possible that a few hardy species, the last of their kind in the world, lived for a few million years longer and finally died by some other means. If so, perhaps the Riches or some other scientists will one day happen on fossils of these beasts.

The Fullness of Time

The possible discovery that some dinosaurs survived the great dying would, of course, alter some views currently held about these creatures. But scientists welcome such unexpected finds. The story of dinosaur discovery has featured a relentless series of ideas and theories that remained popular for a while and then had to be altered or discarded because of new evidence. This

Working in the Smithsonian Museum of Natural History, technician Alex Downs chips away at a slab of stone containing several Coelophysis *skeletons.*

Chasmosaurus, *a long-frilled ceratopsian dinosaur, is menaced by the non-dinosaurian* Phobosuchus *(or* Deinosuchus*), whose nearly 50-foot length makes it the largest ancient crocodile yet discovered.*

trial-and-error approach is part of the scientific method, which seeks, through the discovery of evidence, to get at the truth.

Thus, paleontologists search methodically, year after year, century after century, for the truths about dinosaurs. How did these creatures develop? How did they live? How did they meet their end? The continuing and exciting quest for knowledge about dinosaurs is a tribute to the patience, commitment, courage, and brilliant deductions of the fossil hunters. The efforts of these bone detectives, past and present, has shown to humanity the beautiful and frightening splendor of ages long past. As John Wilford puts it:

> The wonder of dinosaurs is not only that they lived so long ago, grew so large, and then became extinct under mysterious circumstances millions of years before humans came on the scene. The wonder also is that the human mind could resurrect the dinosaurs and through this resurrection begin to comprehend the fullness of time and the richness of life.

Glossary

absolute dating: A direct dating method that measures amounts and proportions of radioactive elements in rocks to determine the age of the rocks.

acid rain: Atmospheric water droplets containing high levels of sulfuric or nitric acid.

avian: A bird.

biped: A creature that walks on two legs.

carnivore: A meat-eating animal.

comparative (or relative) dating: An indirect dating method that compares fossils in various ground layers to determine which fossils formed first and are therefore the oldest.

cosmic: Having to do with the cosmos, or universe; often used to describe something in outer space.

Cretaceous period: A subdivision of the Mesozoic era lasting from about 135 to 65 million years ago.

dinosaur: An ancient extinct land reptile that walked upright with its legs beneath its body; by contrast, the legs of lizards, crocodiles, and other reptiles project outward from their sides.

extinction: The death and elimination of an entire plant or animal species.

extraterrestrial: Originating beyond the earth.

field: Outdoor sites where fossils are found; a person digging at such a site is said to be working "in the field."

field methods: Techniques used to find, excavate, date, and preserve fossil specimens.

fossil: The ancient remains or traces of living things.

fossilization: The process by which living things decay and leave behind remains, imprints, or mineralized replicas of themselves.

half-life: The amount of time it takes for half of a given sample of an unstable element to decay.

heart-brain distance: The vertical distance between an animal's heart and its brain.

herbivore: A plant-eating animal.

iridium: A dark, heavy metal plentiful in meteorites but scarce on the earth's surface.

isotope: An unstable form of a chemical element.

Jurassic period: A subdivision of the Mesozoic era lasting from about 200 to 135 million years ago.

K-T event: The mass extinction in which the dinosaurs perished.

mammal: A backboned, warm-blooded, hairy animal that usually gives birth to live young.

Mesozoic era: The "era of middle life," lasting from about 225 to 65 million years ago, in which dinosaurs lived.

nuclear winter: In theory, a global disaster in which dust clouds in the atmosphere block sunlight long enough to significantly lower temperatures and endanger life.

paleontology: The study of ancient lifeforms.

photosynthesis: The process by which green plants combine carbon dioxide from the air, nutrients from the soil, and sunlight to create energy.

plankton: Tiny and very abundant marine animals that constitute the base of the ocean food chain.

plesiosaurs: A group of large marine reptiles (not dinosaurs).

predator: An animal that preys on other animals.

predator-prey ratio: A comparison of the numbers of predators and their prey in a given area.

priority: Official recognition of having been first to discover or invent something.

pterosaurs: A group of ancient featherless flying reptiles (not dinosaurs).

quadruped: A creature that walks on four legs.

radioactive decay: The breakdown of an unstable form of a chemical element through the process of giving off microscopic particles.

reptile: A backboned, cold-blooded animal, bearing scales or horny plates, that usually reproduces by laying eggs.

species: A specific kind of plant or animal.

strata (singular, stratum): Underground clay or rock layers.

theropods: A group of predatory bipedal dinosaurs; for instance, *Tyrannosaurus rex* and *Coelophysis*.

Triassic period: A subdivision of the Mesozoic era lasting from about 225 to 200 million years ago.

tsunami: A large and sometimes destructive sea wave; tsunamis are sometimes called "tidal" waves, although they are caused by such forces as earthquakes and impacting meteorites and not by the tides.

For Further Reading

Roy Chapman Andrews, *All About Dinosaurs.* New York: Random House, 1953.

Author's Note: Although this book is now out-of-date in many respects, it remains a fascinating view of dinosaurs written by one of the last great adventurer-fossil hunters. It is also the work that first introduced many modern scientists and authors, including myself, to dinosaurs. It is still available in some libraries. If you do not find it in the stacks, ask your librarian if there is a copy in the basement or ask to borrow it from another library.

Isaac Asimov, *Counting the Eons.* New York: Avon Books, 1983.

————, *Did Comets Kill the Dinosaurs?* Milwaukee, WI: G. Stevens Publishing, 1988.

Robin Bates and Cheryl Simon, *The Dinosaurs and the Dark Star.* New York: Macmillan, 1985.

Michael Benton, *Dinosaur and Other Prehistoric Fact Finder.* Phoenix, AZ: Kingfisher Books, 1992.

Jane Burton, *Hunting the Dinosaurs.* Milwaukee, WI: G. Stevens Publishing, 1987.

Dougal Dixon, *Dinosaurs: A Closer Look.* Columbus, OH: Highlights for Children, 1993.

Jerome Goyallon, *Drawing Dinosaurs.* New York: Sterling Publishing, 1993.

Alvin Granowsky, *Dinosaurs of All Sizes.* Austin, TX: Steck-Vaughn, 1992.

Christopher Lampton, *Dinosaurs and the Age of Reptiles.* New York: Watts, 1983.

Jane Mason, *Jurassic Park: The Movie Storybook.* New York: Grosset and Dunlop, 1993.

Julian May, *The Warm-Blooded Dinosaurs.* New York: Holiday House, 1978.

Don Nardo, *The Extinction of the Dinosaurs.* San Diego: Lucent Books, 1994.

Mary Le Duc O'Neill, *Dinosaur Mysteries.* Mahwah, NJ: Troll Associates, 1989.

Gregory S. Paul, "Life Styles of the Big and Hungry," *Science Digest,* April/May 1990.

Lucille R. Penner, *Dinosaur Babies.* New York: Random House, 1991.

James Richardson, *Science Dictionary of Dinosaurs.* Mahwah, NJ: Troll Associates, 1992.

Wilda S. Ross, *What Did the Dinosaurs Eat?* New York: Coward, McCann, and Geoghegan, 1972.

Seymour Simon, *The Largest Dinosaurs.* New York: Macmillan, 1986.

Wendy Stein, *Dinosaurs.* San Diego: Greenhaven Press, 1994.

Robin West, *Dinosaur Discoveries: How to Create Your Own Prehistoric World.* Minneapolis, MN: Carolrhoda Books, 1989.

Peter Zallinger, *Dinosaurs and Other Archosaurs.* New York: Random House, 1986.

Works Consulted

Luis W. Alvarez et al., "Extraterrestrial Cause for the Cretaceous-Tertiary Extinction," *Science*, vol. 208, 1980.

Walter Alvarez and Frank Asaro, "An Extraterrestrial Impact," *Scientific American*, October 1990.

Isaac Asimov, *A Choice of Catastrophes*. New York: Simon and Schuster, 1979.

Robert T. Bakker, *The Dinosaur Heresies*. New York: William Morrow and Company, 1986.

M. J. Benton, "Late Triassic Extinctions and the Origin of the Dinosaurs," *Science*, May 7, 1993.

Edwin Harris Colbert, *Dinosaurs: An Illustrated History*. Maplewood, NJ: Hammond, 1983.

Dougal Dixon et al., *The Macmillan Illustrated Encyclopedia of Dinosaurs and Prehistoric Animals: A Visual Who's Who of Prehistoric Life*. New York: Macmillan, 1988.

W. Glen, "What Killed the Dinosaurs?" *American Scientist*, July/August 1990.

Donald Goldsmith, *Nemesis: The Death Star and Other Theories of Mass Extinction*. New York: Berkeley Books, 1985.

Rick Gore, "Extinctions," *National Geographic*, June 1989.

Stephen Jay Gould, *Bully for Brontosaurus: Reflections in Natural History*. New York: W. W. Norton, 1991.

John R. Horner, *Digging Dinosaurs*. New York: Workman Publishing, 1988.

Kenneth J. Hsu, *The Great Dying*. New York: Ballantine Books, 1986.

Richard A. Kerr, "A Bigger Death Knell for the Dinosaurs?" *Science*, September 17, 1993.

David Lambert, *A Field Guide to Dinosaurs*. New York: Avon Books, 1983.

Don Lessem, *Kings of Creation: How a New Breed of Scientists Is Revolutionizing Our Understanding of Dinosaurs*. New York: Simon and Schuster, 1992.

Richard Monastersky, "Reining in a Galloping *Triceratops*," *Science News*, October 20, 1990.

Virginia Morell, "How Lethal Was the K-T Impact?" *Science*, September 17, 1993.

David Norman, *When Dinosaurs Ruled the Earth*. Santa Monica: Exeter Books, 1985.

——, *The Illustrated Encyclopedia of Dinosaurs*. New York: Crescent Books, 1985.

Byron Preiss and Robert Silverberg, eds., *The Ultimate Dinosaur*. New York: Bantam Books, 1992.

David M. Raup, *Extinction: Bad Genes or Bad Luck?* New York: W. W. Norton, 1991.

Patricia V. Rich and Thomas H. Rich, "Australia's Polar Dinosaurs," *Scientific American*, July 1993.

J. S. Trefil, "Craters, the Terrestrial Calling Cards," *Smithsonian*, September 1989.

Tom Waters, "Cretaceous Splashdown," *Discover*, September 1990.

John Noble Wilford, *The Riddle of the Dinosaur*. New York: Vintage Books, 1985.

——, "For Dinosaur Extinction Theory, a 'Smoking Gun,'" *The New York Times*, February 7, 1991.

Index

absolute dating, 33
Academy of Natural Sciences (Philadelphia), 25
acid rain, 73
Africa, 35
Alaska, 80
Albertosaurus, 31
Allosaurus, 29, 81
    hunting by, 49, 79
Alvarez, Luis, 71-72
Alvarez, Walter, 71-72
American Museum of Natural History (New
    York), 33, 35
Andrews, Roy Chapman, 35-40, 41
Anning, Mary, 17
Antarctica, 80
Apatosaurus, 28
Archaeopteryx, 54-55
    flight of, 51-53, 58
Asia, 24
    see also China
Australia, 80-81
autos,
    on expeditions, 36, 38

Bakker, Robert, 75
    warm-bloodedness and, 43-45, 48-50, 63
Baluchitherium, 37
Belgium, 31
Bible, 13-14
bipedal dinosaurs, 20, 43, 53, 54-55
    evolution of flight and, 56-58
birds, 43, 45, 61-62, 67
    bird-dinosaur link, 51-56, 57-58, 77-78
Bock, Walter J., 57-58
bones,
    debates about, 22-29, 32
    formation of fossils, 24
Boynton, William, 73
brains
    heart-brain distance, 48
    size, 69-71, 78
Bridger Basin, Wyoming, 27
Brontosaurus, 28
Brown, Barnum, 33
Buckland, William, 17, 20, 21

Camarasaurus, 29
camels,
    on expeditions, 36
Canada, 24, 31, 33
Caple, Gerald, 56-58
Caribbean Sea, 75
Carnegie Museum, 32

carnivores, 29, 39, 46-47
    in nuclear winter, 72
    see also hunting; *specific species*
catastrophes
    extinction and, 16, 71-75
ceratopsians. *See Protoceratops*; *Triceratops*
Chasmosaurus, 83
Chatterjee, Sankar, 55-56
Chicxulub (crater), 75
China, 35-40
climate
    change in, 71
    evolution of feathers and, 57
Coelophysis, 54, 64
    warm-bloodedness and, 42-43, 45
Colbert, Edwin H., 42-43, 46
cold-bloodedness. *See* warm-bloodedness
Cold Look at the Warm-Blooded Dinosaurs, 50
collarbones, 53-54
collision, cosmic, 71-75
Colorado, 27
comet, 71-75
Como Bluff, Wyoming, 27, 32
competition,
    among fossil hunters, 22-29
Compsognathus, 53, 54
Conan Doyle, Arthur, 19
continental drift, 74
Cope, Edward Drinker
    competition with Marsh, 22-29
    contributions of, 29-31, 42-43
Corythosaurus, 33, 75
crater, of meteorite, 72, 73-75
Cretaceous period, 10, 70
    extinction in, 68-69
    life in, 33, 66-67
crocodiles, 11, 83
Cuba, 73-75
Currie, Philip, 66
Cuvier, Baron Georges
    as dinosaur expert, 17-18, 20, 21
    extinction theories of, 15-16

dating
    comparative, 30-31
    errors in, 13-14, 17-18
    relative, 30-31
defenses, 62-64
    horns used as, 35, 65
Deinonychus, 45-48, 50
    hunting by, 64, 65
    intelligence of, 71, 77
Digging Dinosaurs (Horner), 61, 65

Dilophosaurus, 64
Dinosaur Cove (Australia), 80
Dinosaur Heresies (Bakker), 44, 48-49
Dinosaur National Monument (Utah), 32
dinosaurs, 33, 71-73
　adaptations of, 74, 80-82
　bird-dinosaur link, 51-58, 77-78
　definitions of, 10-11, 21
　discovery of species, 12, 29, 76
Diplodocus, 29
Douglass, Earl, 32
dragons,
　teeth of, 14
Dryptosaurus, 57
duckbills
　defenses of, 62, 65, 66
　Maiasaurus, 61

Earth
　age of, 13-14, 30
eggs, 61
　eaten by mammals, 69
　first discovery of, 39, 40
Elasmosaurus, 26, 69
Ends of the Earth (Andrews), 35
Europe, 24
evolution
　convergent, 54-55
　of birds, 51-58
　of dinosaurs, 74
expeditions, 27, 36-40, 42
　funding for, 24, 25, 29, 76
extinction
　of dinosaurs, 81-82
　　collision theory, 71-75
　　religious theories, 13-16
　　theories about, 68-71
Extinction: Bad Genes or Bad Luck (Raup), 72

feathers, 51-53, 56-58
feet, 46-47, 53, 55
fingers, 55
fires, after meteorite, 73
"Flaming Cliffs," 37-38, 39-40
flight
　evolution of, 56-58
food, 17
　in nuclear winter, 72
footprints, 24, 80
　of bipeds, 53, 64
forelimbs, 55, 56-58
fossils, 12
　assumptions from 13, 18

care of, 30, 31
dating of, 29-31
formation of, 24
locating, 78
funding, 76, 79
　for fossil hunting, 22, 23-26, 28-29, 36, 40

gases, poisonous, 64
Germany, 51
Gillette, David, 78-79
Gobi Desert, 35-40
governments, 38
　funding for paleontology, 23, 28-29, 40, 76
Granger, Walter, 36-37
Great Exhibition of the Works of Industry
　of All Nations (1851 world's fair), 19
Great Flood, in extinction theories, 14-15

Hadrosaurus, 25
haversian tissue, 48
Hawkins, Benjamin Waterhouse, 19
hearts
　activity levels and, 45
　heart-brain distance, 48
Heilmann, Gerhard, 53-54
herbivores, 18, 20, 24-25
　migrations of, 64
　in nuclear winter, 72
　social behavior of, 61-64
　see also specific species
herding behavior, 63-64, 65-66
Hildebrand, Alan, 73
hindlimbs. *See* legs
hips, 55, 67
horned dinosaurs. *See Protoceratops*;
　Triceratops
Horner, John, 60-64, 65, 66
horns,
　uses of, 35, 65
Hsu, Kenneth J., 75
humans
　fossils of, 36
hunting, 11
　activity levels in, 43, 45, 46-47
　at nesting colonies, 62-63
　development of flight and, 57-58
　in packs, 41, 64-65, 77-78
Huxley, Thomas Henry, 53
Hylaeosaurus, 19, 20, 21

Ichthyosaurus, 17, 73
Iguanodon, 17-18, 19, 21
　posture of, 18, 31

intelligence, 77-78
Iren Dabasu, 37, 38-39
iridium, at K-T boundary, 71-72

jaws
  of *Megalosaurus*, 21
  of *Mosasaurus*, 15-16
jumping
  flight and, 57
Jurassic Park (movie), 19
Jurassic period, 10, 33, 70

K-T boundary, 68-69
King Kong (movie), 19
Kings of Creation (Lessem), 66-67

layers of rock. *See* strata, rock
legs
  birdlike, 43
  forelimbs, 55-58
  speed and, 44
Leidy, Joseph, 24-26
Lessem, Don, 66-67
Lightfoot, John, 14
Linnaeus, Carolus, 14
lizards
  posture of, 21
  similarity of *Iguanodon* to, 18
  structure of hips of, 67
Lost World, The (Conan Doyle), 19
Lyell, Charles, 20-21

Maiasaurus, 61, 63-64, 66
Makela, Bob, 60-63
mammals, 37
  coexistence with dinosaurs, 10, 39-40, 68-69
Mantell, Gideon, 17-20, 21
marine reptiles, 15-16, 17
  after meteorite, 69, 73
Marsh, Othniel Charles
  competition with Cope, 22-29
  contributions of, 29-31
Martin, Larry, 55
mass graves, 63-64
Megalosaurus, 19, 20, 21
Mesozoic era, 10, 33, 39-40
meteorite, as K-T event, 71-75
Mexico, 73-75
Meyer, Grant E., 45-46
Meyer, Hermann von, 51-52
migrations, 64, 74, 80
models, of dinosaurs, 19, 22, 74
Mongolia, 35-40

Monoclonius, 33, 39
Montana, 24-25, 60-61
Morell, Virginia, 73
Mosasaurus, 15-16, 73
movies, about dinosaurs, 19
mudstone, 60

naming, new species, 12, 26-28, 29, 76
nests, 39, 60-63
New Mexico, 79
Noah
  the Great Flood and, 14-15
Norman, David, 55
nuclear winter
  after meteorite, 72-73
  polar dinosaurs in, 81-82

oceans, after meteorite, 73
Origin of Birds, The (Heilmann), 53-54
Ornithiscians, 67
Osborn, Henry Fairfield, 36, 38
Ostrom, John
  bird-dinosaur link and, 51, 54-55
  warm-bloodedness and, 45-48, 50
Oviraptor, 39, 40
Owen, Richard, 21, 31
  dinosaur models and, 19, 22
Oxfordshire (England), 12, 14-15

paleontology
  beginning of, 20-21
  changes in, 22, 40-41, 42
  competition in, 22-29, 32
  debates in, 47-50, 51, 53-56, 69-71
  errors in, 26, 27-28, 32
  methods in, 29-30, 31, 76-77, 78-79
parasites, 75
Phobosuchus, 83
plants
  after meteorite, 72
  for hadrosaurs, 25
plesiosaurs, 11, 69
Plot, Robert, 14-15
polar dinosaurs, 80-82
posture, 11, 21, 53
  of *Iguanodon*, 18, 19, 31
  warm-bloodedness and, 44, 46-47, 48
predators
  predator-prey ratios, 44, 48-50
  see also hunting
priority (official recognition of discovery), 26-28
Protoavis, 55-56
Protoceratops

care of young, 40, 59
  Triceratops and, 38, 39
Pteranodon, 69
Pterodactyl, 16
pterosaurs, 11, 51-53

radar, for locating fossils, 78
radioactivity, in rocks, 33-34
Raup, David M., 72
Red Deer River (Alberta, Canada), 33
religion
  extinction theories and, 13-16
reptiles, 54, 59, 72
  cold-bloodedness of, 43, 45, 46-47
  compared to dinosaurs, 10-11, 11, 21, 48
  flying, 16
revisionism (changes in assumptions), 42-43, 65,
  66-67
Rich, Patricia and Thomas, 81-82
rocks, 33-34, 60
  see also strata, rock
Russell, Dale A., 74

Saurischians, 67
Sauropods. *See Apatosaurus; Seismosaurus*
scientists, 20-21, 22
  agreement of, 58, 73
  beliefs about extinction and, 13-14, 16
Séguin, Ron, 74
Seismosaurus, 78-79
sexual attraction, 65, 66
size
  of *Allosaurus*, 29
  brain, 78
  of *Coelophysis*, 43
  of *Compsognathus*, 53
  of crater, 72
  of *Deinonychus*, 47
  of dinosaurs, 10, 21
  of *Diplodocus*, 29
  of *Megalosaurus*, 20
  of meteorite, 72
  of *Seismosaurus*, 78-79
  of *Velociraptor*, 41
  speed and, 44
social behavior, 59, 62-63, 66-67
sounds, for communication, 65-66
speed
  of dinosaurs, 43, 44
  of meteorite, 72
spine, of *Hylaeosaurus*, 20
Stegosaurus, 29
Stenonychosaurus, 74, 77

Sternberg, Charles H., 33
strata, rock
  dating fossils and, 30-31, 33
  fossils in, 17, 27
Syntarsus, 64

teeth, 61
  fossil, 12, 14
  of *Iguanodon*, 17-18
temperature
  in Australia, 80
  after meteorite, 72, 73
tertiary period, 68-69
Texas, 55-56
theropods, 64-65
  birds and, 54-55, 56-58
tidal waves, 72-73
Trachodon, 24-25
Triassic period, 10, 33, 70
Triceratops
  ancestor of, 38
  discovery of, 29
  galloping of, 44
  uses of horns by, 35, 65
Troödon, 76
tsunamis, 72-73
Two Medicine Formation (Montana), 60-61
Tylosaurus, 69
Tyrannosaurus rex, 54
  hunting by, 64, 78

United States, 24, 73, 75
  paleontology in, 27, 32
  see also specific states
Urey, Harold C., 71
Ussher, James, 13-14
Utah, 32

Velociraptor, 39, 41, 59
volcanoes, 64, 72

warm-bloodedness
  activity levels and, 43-45, 46-47
  debate about, 47-50
  dinosaurs in cold climates and, 81
  growth rate and, 63
Wilford, John, 13-14, 66
Wilson, Woodrow, 32
wings, 16, 56-57
wishbones, 53-54
Wyoming, 27
young, care of, 59, 60-63

About the Author

■■

Don Nardo is an award-winning author whose more than fifty books cover a wide range of topics. His five studies of American wars include *The War of 1812* and *The Persian Gulf War*, and among his overviews of environmental issues are *Ozone*, *Population*, and *Oil Spills*. He has also produced a number of health-related works, including *Medical Diagnosis*, *Anxiety and Phobias*, *Drugs and Sports*, and *Vitamins and Minerals*. Mr. Nardo has a degree in history, and among his history studies are *Ancient Greece*, *The Roman Empire*, *Greek and Roman Theater*, *Traditional Japan*, and *Braving the New World*. In a related vein, his biographies of historical figures include books on Cleopatra, Charles Darwin, Thomas Jefferson, H. G. Wells, and Franklin D. Roosevelt. Among the other Lucent Encyclopedia of Discovery and Invention titles by Mr. Nardo are: *Lasers*, *Animation*, *Germs*, *Gravity*, *Computers*, and *Vaccines*. In addition, he has written *The Extinction of the Dinosaurs* for young children and numerous screenplays and teleplays, including work for Warner Brothers and ABC Television. Mr. Nardo lives with his wife, Christine, on Cape Cod, Massachusetts.

Picture Credits